D0099023

THE ODD SQUAD

ZERO TOLERANCE

MICHAEL FRY

THE ODD SQUAD

ZERO TOLERANCE

Disney · HYPERION BOOKS
· NEW YORK ·

First Edition

1 3 5 7 9 10 8 6 4 2

G475-5664-5-12336

Printed in the United States of America

Library of Congress Cataloging-in-Publication Data

Fry, Michael 1959–
The Odd Squad: zero tolerance / by Michael Fry.—First U.S. edition.
pages cm.
Summary: Simone, a new student, seems intent on stealing Molly away from Nick and the only way Nick can think to stop her is by teaming with his old anti-bullying ally, but that will require Nick using himself as bait—both as the bullied and bullier.

ISBN 978-1-4231-7099-0

[1. Middle schools—Fiction. 2. Schools—Fiction. 3. Bullies—Fiction. 4. Interpersonal relations—Fiction.] I. Title. II. Title: Zero tolerance.
PZ7.F9234Oem 2013
[Fic]—dc23   2013001972

Reinforced binding

Visit www.disneyhyperionbooks.com
www.disney.com/theoddsquad

TO SARAH AND EMILY

CHAPTER 1

T all," I said.

"No, what do you *really* want to be when you grow up?" said Molly.

Molly, Karl, and I were standing outside school after a fire drill, doing our Safety Patrol thing. We were supposed to be looking for stragglers, but mostly, we were just trying not to look stupid.

"Or raise sloths," Karl continued. "Did you know they only go to the bathroom once a week?"

It wasn't going well.

Everyone at Emily Dickinson Middle School still calls us the Loser Patrol, even though we saved the school from a bully named Roy.

But that was a few weeks ago. Which is like three years in middle school time.

"I used to want to be a zombie," said Karl.

When Karl is being weird, Molly and I stare at him until he stops.

Karl continued, "But then I found out you have to die first."

When staring doesn't work, we ignore him.

Karl sighed. "My mom would never sign the permission slip."

When ignoring Karl doesn't work, we stare at him again and growl.

Karl took out his phone. "At least I don't think so. Maybe I should call her and ask."

When staring and growling don't work, Molly takes over.

"ENOUGH!" she yelled.

"AHHH!" screamed Karl.

Molly reached for Karl. "I'm sorry. I didn't mean to—"

"Not you! THAT!" said Karl as he pointed to a flapping plastic grocery bag stuck to the grass. "It's on the list!"

The list is Karl's List of Fears. He wrote them all out on paper for Molly and me to check when he's being weird—which is pretty much all the time, because he's pretty much afraid of everything.

KARL'S LIST OF FEARS
1. HEIGHTS
2. COSTUMED CHARACTERS (STEAL YOUR SOUL!)
3. FLYING PLASTIC BAGS (EVIL!)
4. WICKED WITCH OF WEST (DUH.)
5. ANTIQUE FURNITURE (JUST CREEPY)
6. GIANT SQUID (THEY'RE GIANT!)
7. MUMMIES (ONLY REAL ONES)
8. PLATYPUSES (FURRY DUCKS?)

Karl slowly backed away. "Plastic bags are alive. Any second they could blow into your face and choke you to death!"

Molly stifled a laugh. "It's not alive, Karl."

I was about to laugh too, just before a gust of wind came up and the bag attacked me.

Karl started walking back to class. He looked back. "Still want to be tall?"

Molly shook her head. She had that look, the I-can't-wait-to-grow-up-and-forget-I-was-ever-twelve look.

I thought, Good luck with that. Freakishly odd friends are better than no friends at all. I know. I used to not have any friends. It was okay. . . .

But not really.

Now we're all friends because the school
counselor, Dr. Daniels, forced the three of us to
join Safety Patrol to cure our "peer allergies."
Which turned out great in the end. Although
I wish Molly and Karl had come with warning
labels.

Molly can be loud and bossy. And it's gotten worse since our advisor (and school janitor) Mr. Dupree made her Safety Patrol captain. Karl and I call her Captain Bossy Pants.

The problem with having a Captain Bossy Pants these days is there isn't a lot for her to be bossy about. The only reason we all joined Safety Patrol was to stop Roy. Now that he's retired, there's no more bullying.

With no more bullying, Safety Patrol has become pretty boring.

Boring or not, Safety Patrol still got us out of class. But we couldn't stay out forever, and it was time Molly and I headed back. We hadn't gone three steps when we noticed Karl stopped ahead of us. He was pointing at the sidewalk.

"What's the matter with him?" I asked.

Molly eyed me. "Is that a trick question?"

But it wasn't just Karl being Karl. When we caught up we realized it's kind of hard not to stare at the sidewalk when . . .

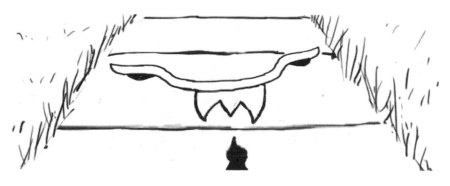

. . . it's staring back at you.

$\mathcal{I}$t was some sort of chalk drawing.

It didn't look like anything I'd seen before—at least on Earth.

"It looks sort of like the Swamp Shifter from *NanoNerd* #75," I said.

Karl walked around the drawing and studied it upside down (or right

side up?). He smiled. "I know what this is. It's a Swedish cheese grater!"

"A what?" I said.

"From UMakia," said Karl. "My parents go there all the time to buy throw pillows. Mom loves throw pillows. I don't know about Dad. He just holds her purse and stares at his shoes." He nodded. "I'm not afraid of cheese graters."

Karl's ringtone went off.

"Hi, Mom. What? . . . That's great! . . . I'm so relieved! . . . Love you too. Bye."

Karl hung up. "Great news! Mom found my sea monkeys' volleyball net under the cushions of the couch!"

Molly started to say something, then stopped. She turned to me. "It's not a Swamp Shifter or a cheese grater. It looks to me like some sixth grader's scribble."

"It could be a message," I said.

Molly shook her head. "Don't go there."

"It could!"

"Nick, it isn't."

"How else do you explain—"

"Coincidence," said Molly.

"On second thought, it could be a carrot peeler," said Karl.

"It's not," said Molly.

That's when I dug into my pocket for the Tater Tot I'd been saving since lunch. I popped it in my mouth and started chewing. "I 'on't mow. I 'eally 'ink it's—"

When you almost sort of die choking on a Tot, it takes a few minutes to get your breath back and figure out what you're going to say to the person who sort of saved your life.

"Yeah, I'm okay," I said. "Thanks for . . . you know . . ."

"No. No problem. I shouldn't have yelled and made you choke."

"I'm good."

"Right. Okay."

Molly and I stared at each other for a few seconds and tried not to say anything too icky/ creepy that we would later have to swear we never said. Fortunately, we were interrupted.

CHAPTER 3

We turned around. In front of us was a girl dressed in black. Black jeans, black shirt, black hair, and black hat. We stared. She stared back.

Finally Karl asked, "Is this a staring contest? I once stared at my parakeet, Stanley, for seven hours." Karl paused. "He was never really the same after that."

The girl stuck out her hand and announced in a thick French accent, "Hello. I am Simone."

I said, "Are you . . . ?

"French? *Oui!*" She nodded. "My family just moved here."

Karl grabbed Simone's hand and started shaking it way too hard.

16

I took pity on her and pried Karl's hand away. "I'm Nick. And this is Molly."

Molly took a couple steps back. "Hey," she whispered.

Simone looked up at Molly. "You are so . . . how you say? High?"

"Tall," sighed Molly. "I'm freakishly tall."

"No, no! *Très magnifique!* Is amazing! You are a model, *oui?*"

I snorted, then instantly regretted it after Molly pounded me in the shoulder. Hard. All that freakish height allows her to pick up a lot of speed.

"That hurt," I whined.

"Good," she said.

I glared at Molly. "*Vous êtes une pomme de terre avec le visage d'un cochon d'Inde.*"

"What did you just say?"

"He said, 'You are a potato with the face of a guinea pig,'" said Simone.

"Whoa," said Karl.

"Take that back!" said Molly as she targeted my shoulder with her fist again.

"Okay, okay," I said. "You don't look like a potato."

"Did you know that guinea pigs eat their own poop?" asked Karl. "They can't digest their food the first time. Isn't that cool?"

We all stared at Karl.

Simone looked at me. "*Vous parlez français?*"

She was asking if I spoke French. I was certainly *taking* French. But all that had stuck was one insult (see above) and my name in French (Nick).

French is hard. It's like yogacize for your tongue.

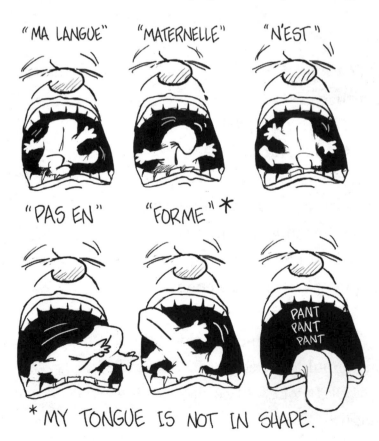

* MY TONGUE IS NOT IN SHAPE.

I played it safe. I answered Simone's question with my go-to play-it-safe move. I shrugged.

Simone smiled. *"Votre glissière est en panne."*

"Huh?"

Simone pointed to my pants. "Your zipper. It is down."

I looked down. My zipper was up.

Molly laughed. "Made you look!"

"Très funny," I said.

"It *was* funny. Know why?" Karl nodded as he zipped up his own pants. "Because it's not happening to me."

Molly smiled at Simone. "Let me take you to the office, where you can register."

"Oui, oui, that would be, how you say, awesome? But first, who is this Emily you were shouting about?"

"She's real," I said.

Molly rolled her eyes. "She's someone kids made up years ago to explain stuff that can't be explained. Like why the pencil sharpener eats your pencils or why there's always one burnt Tot in the bunch."

Simone nodded. "Oh, I see. This Emily, she is a myth, then."

Molly looked at me. "That's exactly what she is."

Emily is not a myth. Emily is real. At least, I think she's real. Or I'm pretty sure she's real. Okay, she might not be real.

It's complicated.

A few weeks back, we went up against Roy. He was big and mean and smelled like ripe bananas (Fiesta Mist Body Spray).

Things got a little crazy.

I used my grandmother's phone to pretend I was someone else so I could text-torture Roy and steal the stuffed pig his mom got him (before she left). When I discovered I had become just as much of a bully as Roy, I helped him get his pig back after a pet python was released during a science fair, which caused the crowd to stampede . . . just before Roy and I fell out of the ceiling and pretty much destroyed the cafetorium. Over a few weeks of detention we worked things out, and everyone lived slightly happier ever after.

Oh, and the python is fine.

But during all that, some seriously weird stuff happened that I can't explain. Like . . .

SOMEONE... DISTRACTED EVERYONE WHEN WE NEEDED TO ESCAPE.

RECEIVED MASS TEXT TO LOOK UP.

LOOKING UP.

SOMEONE... HELPED US FIND OUR WAY WHEN WE WERE LOST.

HAD HIS PHONE OFF

THEN WHOSE LIGHT DID HE SEE?

SOMEONE... CAME TO OUR RESCUE OVER AND OVER AGAIN WHEN OUR BACKS WERE AGAINST THE WALL.

RUNNING FROM PET PYTHON...

...RELEASED DURING THE SCIENCE FAIR BY ?

Pretty much whenever we needed help, we got it. But I could never figure out who was helping us.

That leaves Emily. And by Emily I don't mean the imaginary person everyone thinks she is. She's NOT a ghost!

She's a real person. Someone who knows the school, doesn't want to be found, and for some reason is on our side.

"I think she's real," I said as I pointed to the sidewalk. "And I think this drawing could be a message from her . . . or him . . . or whatever."

21

Karl said, "You know, it could be a Julianne fry maker."

I said, "It's not a—"

"Why are they called Julianne fries?" asked Karl. "Who is Julianne? Why are they zigzaggy? Does her hand shake when she makes them?" He gasped. "Is Julianne sick?!"

I said, "Stop talking, Karl."

Molly and Simone shared one of those all-boys-are-aliens looks. Mom and Memaw give me that look a lot. Especially when I let our dog, Janice, lick peanut butter off my toes.

As I watched Molly and Simone walk to the office like they were old friends it started to bug me. I mean, Simone is new. And new kids are all nice at first. They have to be. They're NEW!

It's just that you don't know who they really are. You don't know what they'll do when you really need them. Like . . . when you choke on a Tot!

I mean, if Molly chokes, is Simone going to whack her back? It took Molly and me weeks to get where we would whack each other's back. You have to earn a whack on the back. You don't just throw back whacks around like they're nothing!

"Back whacks don't come cheap!" I said accidentally out loud.

"What?" said Karl.

"Never mind."

"Simone seems nice," said Karl.

"She's okay, I guess."

"I wish I were from France."

"What?"

"If I were from France, everybody would be like, 'What's it like to be from France?' And I'd say, 'It's sort of like here except everyone speaks French, and hardly anyone is ever attacked by a plastic bag.' And they'd say, 'Whoa!' And then everyone would come over to my house and watch my sea monkeys play volleyball."

"Karl, you're so weird."

"I know. My mom says it'll pay off one day."

CHAPTER 4

By the end of the day I had forgotten all about Simone and Swamp Shifters and cheese graters.

I had bigger problems.

My French teacher, Madame Alamode, asked me to stay after class.

Madame Alamode is creepily awesome. The only reason I'm in her class is to watch her slice fruit for her lunch with her scale-model guillotine.

"Nick, I want to discuss the D you received on your paper on common French phrases," she said. "*Ma cuisse me démange* is not a common French phrase, and neither is *Ne manges pas mes ongles de pieds!*"

I don't know about her house, but in mine those two phrases are pretty much daily conversation.

Madame Alamode continued, "Nick, your grades have really been slipping. If you don't get your grade up to a B in the next three weeks, you won't be able to go on the class field trip."

I freaked. "What? No!"

Every year all the seventh graders not on academic probation go on a Saturday field trip to King Potatamus's Egyptopolis (and Water Park). It's an Egyptian-themed water park with a bunch of fake pyramids along a fake Nile River with lots of fake animals fake-tearing each other apart.

The park's spokes-character is King Potatamus, a hip-hop hippopotamus that stars in all their commercials.

The field trip is supposed to be educational because we're all working on our Egypt unit in World History, but it's mostly just a chance to overdose on sugar, get soaked, and throw up soggy pizza.

I HAVE TO GO! It's the best field trip of the year. I mean, I'll bet even Roy and his Future Inmates of America buddies will get to go (I heard they get credit in English for stuff like spelling *great* with an 8). If I'm not there, everyone will know I'm failing. I'll become That Kid Who Didn't Go on That Field Trip That Even Roy Went On!

Then I'll have to go into the Kid Protection Program like that *other* kid at that *other* school who accidentally set their clothes *and* their trying-to-help principal on fire during an honors assembly. Everyone's okay. But the kid had to move to Guam to escape the shame.

Seriously, it happened. I read it on the Internet.

But the *real* reason I had to go was I just maybe might possibly finally be tall enough to ride the world's tallest zip-line ride: the Flying Pyramid.

There seriously was a chance . . . *if* I grew an inch and a half in the next three weeks.

It could happen.

Madame Alamode pointed to the door. "I've arranged for a French II student to help you."

Holy beans! It was Becky Harrison, my sort-of friend who happens to be a girl I can only kind of talk to without tying my tonsils into a knot.

28

Kind of.

Madame Alamode sighed. "Maybe we should start with English and work our way up to French."

Becky giggled. She giggled perfectly. Like she does everything perfectly. Walking. Talking. Breathing. Blinking. Gum twirling . . .

Wait. Gum twirling?!

There's a really good reason Becky's gum gift freaked me out. When I was little, I found a wad of gum under a swing.

I peeled it off, popped it in my mouth, and started chewing. It wasn't bad. It still had a lot of flavor.

That's when my mom screamed. It wasn't a typical mom freak-out scream. It was more like a vampire-squid-is-eating-my-baby scream.

My mom's a nurse, so she knows gum is full of toxic germs that can turn your insides to slush. She acted fast.

Ever since that day, even the sight of used gum can cause me to barf, resulting in an out-of-body experience.

Fortunately, when Becky offered me her gum I didn't throw up. Because when I pushed past her to escape, I got distracted by Mr. Dupree outside.

He was hosing off the sidewalk! He was ERASING Emily's chalk drawing!

I ran down the hall and out the front doors and grabbed the hose from him. "You can't erase it!" I said.

He pointed to the drawing. "What? That?"

Becky ran up. "What's going on?"

"It means something," I said.

"It looks like a monster," said Becky. "Or maybe a—"

"Cheese grater?" suggested Mr. Dupree.

"It's not a cheese grater," I said. "It's a message."

"From whom?" asked Mr. Dupree.

"Emily!" said Becky.

"Not Emily," I said. "I mean, not the Emily who's not real. Wait. I mean, the Emily who *is* real. No. I mean, the Emily who someone's pretending might be real." I nodded. "THAT'S who I mean."

Mr. Dupree shook his head. "'All that glisters is not gold.'"

"Glisters?" said Becky.

"It's Shakespeare," I explained. "Mr. Dupree uses it in Safety Patrol to annoy us. And no, I don't know what it means."

"It means things are not always what they seem," said Mr. Dupree. "Which reminds me of a story from when I was a zookeeper. Want to hear it?"

Becky looked to me. I said, "He's not asking for permission. Just ignore—"

"One day we were painting the elephant enclosure," said Mr. Dupree. "At some point we noticed that one of the females, Martha, had picked

32

up a brush with her trunk and painted something on the wall.

"No one could agree on what she was drawing, but it seemed clear Martha was trying to communicate something. So I got Martha some canvases and her own paints and let her communicate to her heart's content.

"People came to watch. Lots of people.

"Martha's paintings started selling for lots of money. She became famous.

"One day I looked a little closer as Martha painted. I noticed that every time she used the brush she was scratching her trunk with the opposite end. When I inspected her trunk there was a small wound."

POOR GIRL.

I said, "So she—"

"Wasn't really painting?" interrupted Becky.

Mr. Dupree shook his head, "I dressed the wound, the itch went away, and Martha never painted again."

I said, "So she—"

"Wasn't communicating at all!" interrupted Becky again as she stretched a string of gum from her teeth and whipped it around like a mini jump rope.

Not only does she torture gum, she's a repeat interrupter!

"No. She *was* communicating," continued Mr. Dupree. "She was communicating that she had an itchy trunk."

"Ohhhh," said Becky and me at the same time.

I looked down at the drawing and shook my head. "I don't know. Maybe it is a cheese grater."

Mr. Dupree blasted the sidewalk with his hose. "Whatever it is, it's got to go."

"Whatever it is, *we'll* figure it out," said Becky.

We? Did Becky say "we"? She did! She said "WE"!

For exactly seven seconds I forgot about the gum twirling and the interrupting until . . . a gust of wind wrapped Becky's hair around her gum-rope.

And sent me sprinting out of barf range.

CHAPTER 5

When I got home I was still holding my stomach in to keep it from flying out of my mouth. All I wanted to do was go straight upstairs and brush my teeth with shampoo. Memaw had other ideas.

"Check out the new trick I taught Janice," said Memaw.

I shook my head no.

"Who sat in your spaghetti?"

"Nobody," I said.

Memaw shook her head. "A nobody is almost always a somebody that *someone* doesn't want to be just anybody."

"Huh?"

"Give me a name!"

It was no use. Memaw could make a mime scream.

I told her everything.

Memaw shook her head. "I told your mother that her gum freak-out would come back to haunt us."

"What am I supposed to do?"

"Sweetie, life is never a simple skip-to-your-Lou through a mountain meadow. At some point, your underwear's gonna ride up your butt."

I had no idea what that meant.

She continued, "You're going to run into situations where people you like do stuff you hate. Gross happens. Annoying happens. Accidental thongs happen! Don't let it get to you."

"But what if I throw up on her shoes at school in front of everyone and have to enter the Kid Protection Program and move to Guam?"

"The kid what?"

"You know, like *that* kid at *that* school during that honors assembly."

EVERYONE WAS STANDING ON RISERS HOLDING LIT CANDLES.

THEY HAD THIS MOMENT OF SILENCE AND THIS ONE KID FORGOT SHE WAS HOLDING A CANDLE.

"Oh, my," said Memaw. "I'm not sure Guam is far enough away."

"I know!"

Memaw smiled. "In any case, I still think you should tell Becky the truth. If she's a real friend, she'll stop playing with her gum."

"She really likes gum."

"More than she likes you?"

"I don't know. Maybe I can just ignore it."

"Right until you throw up on her shoes?"

I hate when Memaw grills me like this. She's like the bad cop on that show *Justice and Peace*.

"Nobody's perfect, Nick. Not you. Not Becky."

"What about Phil?" I asked.

"Phil isn't perfect either," said Memaw.

"Although he is unusually handsome and extremely polite, and smells like cantaloupe."

Phil is dating my mom. I don't like him. Even though he really does smell like cantaloupe. He also dresses nice, is a good listener, eats all his peas, and does the dishes without being asked. Oh, and he has crazy perfect hair. It doesn't look natural, except it does!

He's too perfect. But not like Becky is too

40

perfect. Or was too perfect. If only Phil liked to share his used gum. Then I could really hate him. But that would mean I'd have to hate Becky too. It was all so confusing.

"By the way," said Memaw, "Phil's coming over for dinner tonight."

"Great," I said as I rolled my eyes.

"Give Phil a chance. And give Becky a chance. People can surprise you."

Maybe, I thought.

But probably not.

CHAPTER 6

Dinner started late because Mom ordered the wrong pizza. Ever since Memaw discovered macaroni-and-cheese pizza, it's the only kind she'll eat. Just like she only eats mac-n-cheese chow mein and mac-n-cheese burritos.

Memaw really likes mac-n-cheese.

When we finally sat down for dinner, my plan was to eat and run without having to be fake-nice to Perfect Phil.

I was almost finished when Mom gave Phil a

nod. Phil turned to me. "So, dude, how's it going at Emily Dickinson these days?"

Phil calling me "dude" was annoying, but not like you'd think it'd be annoying — you know, like an adult trying to be cool. He said it dorky *on purpose.* Which is like saying, *I'm not as cool as you are.* Which is the perfect way to say it to a kid.

Which made it especially annoying.

"Fine," I said.

Phil winked at me. "You know, if you have any trouble with Dr. Daniels, I can have her parking space taken away."

"Ha-ha," I fake-laughed.

Phil works for the school district. I don't know what he does—probably something annoyingly, perfectly cool.

"You know, I was also in Safety Patrol when I was your age," said Phil.

"Wow," I said, a little too sarcastically.

"Yeah, I thought it was mostly lame too, but at least we got out of class a lot, even if the other kids made fun of our belts and badges and called us the Loser Patrol."

43

Gee, I thought, except for the perfect hair, the perfect grin, and the perfect way he talked *up* to kids, Phil was just like me!

Yeah, right.

I finished dinner and asked if I could be excused.

"You may," said Mom. "Do you have homework?"

"Yeah, I've got a French test."

"Très magnifique!" said Phil. *"Je minored en français au université."*

Mom squealed. *"J'étais en Guyane française dans les Corps de la Paix."*

I tried to translate in my head.

I failed.

As soon as I got to my room my phone buzzed.

It was a text from Becky:

Becky: Homework on VidChat?

Uh-oh. What was I supposed to do? On the one hand, Becky is the prettiest girl in school and she used the word *we* right in front of me. On the other hand . . .

. . . I had just eaten.

CHAPTER 7

I sat at my desk and stared at the video chat icon.

Maybe the gum gross-out and the interrupting were onetime things. Maybe she had run out of gum. Maybe the Gum Police had scared her straight.

It could happen.

I clicked on the screen.

Little Miss Smack Attack was back.

"What happened? Are you okay?" asked Becky.

"Just a . . . a little on edge. Sort of stressful day," I said.

"Oh. I guess we can go over things before school instead."

Again with the *WE*!

"Yeah. Let's do that," I said. "Um, Becky?"

"Yeah?"

I was just about to take Memaw's advice and tell her how I really felt, when it became super clear exactly how Becky really felt.

Becky *really* liked her gum. I realized I liked her too much to ask her to give it up. Plus, she might NEVER EVER speak to me again if I did.

"Nothing," I said.

Becky said, "Hey, before you go—I've been thinking about that sidewalk drawing. I think you're right. It really does mean something."

She held up a sketch of the drawing on the screen. "What if each part represents a word? You know, like hieroglyphics."

"Right! Like the ones all over King Potatamus's Egyptopolis."

"And ancient Egypt."

Wait. I knew that. Why wouldn't she think I knew that? I know stuff. I know how to hard-boil an egg in the microwave (three out of five times). I know that a bunch of parrots is called a pandemonium of parrots. I know what NanoNerd wears under his NanoSuit (NanoBriefs!). I know LOTS of stuff. And I was going to tell her that—except she kept talking.

"But they're not hieroglyphics," Becky continued. "I checked online and nothing in the drawing makes any sense."

"But that doesn't mean—"

"—it isn't a simple pictogram."

Again with the interrupting!

Becky looked at her sketch. "Horns-teeth-eyes? Teeth-horn-eyes? Eyes-teeth-horns?"

"Becky?" said a voice offscreen. "Is this *another* cereal bowl growing mold under your bed?"

"I gotta go," said Becky. The screen clicked off.

Terrific. Becky is not only a disgusting gum smacker and an interrupter, she also thinks I don't know stuff I really do know, AND she's a mold farmer!

Then again, she'd said "we" twice. Twice is officially LOTS of times.

I had to weigh the Becky pros and cons very carefully.

With that settled, I decided to look at the drawing again. Wait. What if those aren't teeth? What if the horns mean bull? What if they're . . .

"I EAT BULLIES!"

That's it! That HAS to be it! There really is an Emily, and she really is helping us! I was completely 100 percent totally sure . . .

. . . for two seconds.

CHAPTER 8

Really? You're out of gum?" I said to Becky the next morning in the school library.

"My mom took it away," said Becky. "She says it's disgusting the way I can't keep it in my mouth. Can you believe that?"

Now that Darth Smacker was gone, I could focus on helping Becky with her math.

I used to not be good at math. But then something clicked, and I could just see the answers. Weird, I know. I have to hide it, though. I've got enough working against me with being short and in Safety Patrol. I don't need to be a math nerd too. That's why I'm more of a math ninja.

After I helped Becky, she helped me conjugate the verb "to be" in French.

When the blood returned to my tongue, we checked the chalk drawing on Becky's phone again.

"Bully Watch does make the most sense," I said. "I mean, if it's coming from Emily."

"Have you shown it to anyone else?"

Before I could answer, Karl, Molly, and Simone walked into the library.

THE MODELS ARE SO SKINNY! HOW DO THEY STAY ALIVE?

HAIR CLIPPINGS AND TEARS.

FASHION MAGAZINE

Molly spied the chalk drawing on Becky's phone. "You're still messing with that dumb drawing?"

"We think it means Bully Watch," said Becky.

Another *WE*! That's three *we*s. That's a PANDEMONIUM of *we*'s!

Molly rolled her eyes. "It's not Emily."

I pointed to the phone. "Look at it again. See. Bull-E-Watch. It really could be a message."

Molly shook her head. "You're seeing things.

There isn't some know-it-all superkid out there sending us secret messages."

I said, "How else do you explain—?"

"Maybe it is this Emily. Maybe she is trying to tell us something?" interrupted Simone.

"Really?" I said. "You think so?"

"I do," said Simone. "This Emily, she cannot just tell us what she wants because she is, how you say, shy?"

"She *is* shy," agreed Karl. "She's like my parakeet, Stanley. He won't poop if you're watching him. I've never seen him poop. I know he does. But I've never seen him do it. Never ever."

We all stared at Karl.

Simone moved on. "This Emily, she is so shy no one has ever seen her or heard her."

"Right," I said.

"But she could be watching us anytime, *oui*?"

"I suppose."

"She knows if we're in trouble? She knows if we're safe?"

"Nick," said Becky.

"Just a second," I said.

"She knows if you, how you say, if you are bad? Or not bad?"

55

"That's right." I nodded.

"Nick," said Becky a little louder.

"Not now," I said.

"So you should always be good? For the sake of being good?"

"I guess. What are you trying to say?"

"'You better watch out, you better not cry,'" sang Simone and Molly. "'You better not pout, I'm telling you why—'"

Molly and Simone started laughing. Becky looked at me. "I tried to warn you."

I glared at Molly.

"We're just teasing," said Molly. "Lighten up."

EMILY IS COMING TO TOWN!

I watched Molly and Simone walk off giggling. Back-whacking friends who sort of save your life shouldn't tease you. Back-whacking friends should have each other's back. Unless . . . they have some one else's back. Or something.

Karl said, "Is Santa Claus—?"

"No, Karl. Emily is not Santa Claus. Emily is real," I said.

"Santa Claus is real," said Karl.

I said, "Karl . . ." just as Becky clapped her hand over my mouth.

Becky said, "Yes, Karl. Just like Emily is real. Right, Nick?"

I nodded as Becky removed her gum-smelling hand from my mouth, causing my stomach to do a triple flip into my spleen.

"You know what? I'm going to prove Emily is real," I said.

"How?" asked Becky.

Suddenly it hit me. "She only shows up when we need her!"

"What are you saying?"

"Like, when we're in trouble. Or being bullied."

The bell rang.

Becky gathered up her stuff to go to class as Karl, holding a Tot in his hand, stared at the skinny model on the magazine cover.

I WONDER IF I CAN SEND HER TOTS THROUGH THE MAIL.

"Too bad there aren't any more bullies to lure Emily out," said Becky.

I picked up my backpack. "Yeah, too bad."

I followed Becky and Karl out of the library, then headed to my first-period world history class.

What is Molly's problem? Why is she so down on Emily? She's seen all the same weird stuff Karl and I have. It's like she's ignoring the evidence on purpose.

Or Simone's convinced her I'm an idiot. They've gotten so close so fast it's like Simone's got some sort of dark, evil power over Molly.

I was really worried about Molly. I was! You know . . . when I wasn't worried about myself.

That's when it hit me. If I could prove Emily was real it wouldn't just put Simone back in her new kid place, but it also might get Molly to stop acting all weird and make her come back to my side. You know, the non–Mademoiselle in Black side.

All I had to do was flush Emily out by getting myself bullied when there weren't any bullies. But how?

It seemed hopeless until I walked into World History and instantly got tripped by a huge, hulking kid.

I thought, Hey, I just got bullied! Cool!

But that was before I looked back to see who it was.

False alarm. It was just Warren Pickles, the Your Personal Space Is My Personal Space Boy.

"Warren, what are you wearing?" I asked.

"Remember? It's Egypt week, and I'm a mummy!" Warren explained. "I wrapped me myself. It only took three hours!"

"Awesome. You did it yourself," I said as I
started to get up. Then I stopped and thought . . .

CHAPTER 9

I was the first one at school the next day. I got there so early even Emily was still asleep.

I went straight to the second-floor boys' bathroom to begin Operation Flush Emily Out.

I figured if Emily wasn't real, then Molly and Karl would find me. Either way I'd be fine.

What could possibly go wrong?

I crawled into the trash can. It was empty except for . . .

Gross! It was like being stuck in Becky's mouth. And school didn't start for twenty minutes!

I was sure I wouldn't survive, until I suddenly remembered five magical letters: *WWNND*.

I tried to NanoNerd up and think happy thoughts. But no unicorns or rainbows. Some things are worse than sitting in gum.

After the longest twenty minutes in the history of twenty minutes, I texted Molly and Karl.

Nick: TP'd, stuffed in trash. Don't know where!
    Dark! HELP!

Just as I was about to hit SEND, I heard someone burst into the bathroom, followed by the slam of a stall door.

Someone was barfing up a lung. After about a minute, he stopped, left the stall, and turned the water on at a sink. That's when I hit SEND on the text and immediately heard . . .

He was about to hurl. Again! I had no choice but to rear back and tip the trash can over.

Karl missed me by inches.

When I poked my head out of the trash can, Karl screamed . . .

Karl's kick sent the trash can, with me in it, spinning toward the door—just as it opened. I rolled out of the bathroom and into the hall and straight for the . . .

After I figured out which way was up, I slowly peeked out of the trash can and came face-to-feet with a pair of bright purple women's shoes.

Hurt-your-eyes purple. There's only one person at Emily Dickinson Middle School who wears hurt-your-eyes purple shoes.

I looked up.

Karl rushed down the stairs. "Nick? You KNOW mummies are number four on my list of fears!"

"What list of fears?" asked Dr. Daniels.

"It's not important," I said.

Karl showed Dr. Daniels the list on his phone. "I can text you a copy. Wait. There's a text from Nick. TP'd? Stuffed in trash? Dark? Help?"

"Let me see that," said Dr. Daniels. She looked at the screen, then at me. She slowly shook her head. "In my office, NOW!"

Dr. Daniels walked off, leading the way. I glared at Karl. "What were you doing in the . . ."

Karl's stomach groaned.

CHAPTER 10

It had been a few weeks since I'd been in Dr. Daniels's office. I noticed a new therapy doll and brochure.

I wasn't too worried. I figured she'd ask a bunch of questions and I'd shrug a lot. When all was said and done, no one was actually bullied, right?

Dr. Daniels stopped typing and turned to me. She looked serious—*seriously* serious.

"Who did this to you?" she asked.

I shrugged.

"Nick, you have to tell me."

I shrugged again.

"Nick, you don't understand the situation. After the last bullying incident, the school district has been all over us. If we can resolve this quickly, we can keep them out of it. And we *really* want them out of this."

"Why?" I asked.

The door opened and a familiar voice said, "Have no fear! Zero Tolerance is here!"

I turned. It was Perfect Phil flashing a perfect smile. "Don't worry, little dude. I've got this covered."

"What are you doing here?" asked Dr. Daniels.

"District got an anonymous call that you have another bully," said Phil.

"I have it under control," said Dr. Daniels.

Phil said, "If you had it under control, it would be under control, now wouldn't it?"

"We don't even know what happened yet," said Dr. Daniels. "If you'll just give me some time to—"

Phil turned to me. "Nick, were you bullied?"

Technically, I *had* been bullied. I nodded.

Phil looked back at Dr. Daniels. "Case closed. Now, I'll need some office space and some supplies to set up a ZT program."

"What's ZT?" I asked.

THE ANSWER TO ALL YOUR PROBLEMS.

STILL PERFECT HAIR.

WILL IT MAKE ME TALLER? WILL IT STOP MOLLY FROM BEING ALL WEIRD? WILL IT MAKE BECKY STOP TORTURING GUM?

But I could tell from the look on Dr. Daniels's face that the answer was . . . probably not.

CHAPTER 11

T he next day Karl and I sat together in the
cafetorium with the rest of school as Perfect Phil
announced . . .

ZERO TOLERANCE FOR INTOLERANCE

THE TIME HAS COME FOR BULLYING TO END.

Even though it never really started back up.

Phil continued, "Anyone caught bullying will
be suspended. Automatically. No appeals. No
exceptions. Anyone caught bullying a second time
will be expelled for the remainder of the year."

But that means . . .

"The student will repeat the entire school year," said Phil.

The entire cafetorium gasped. Grade repeaters are social zombies. They're dead to kids who go on to the next grade and dead to kids who come up from a lower grade. Eventually, grade repeaters can become totally invisible.

"We will find the person responsible for this latest bullying incident," said Phil. "The *anonymous* victim has my promise."

Everyone turned to look at Mr. Anonymous.

MR. ANONYMOUS

At that moment I wanted more than anything to disappear through a trapdoor in the floor.

LAND WHERE KIDS CAN HIDE FROM THE STUPID STUFF THEY DO

I never get what I want.

Instead, I had to sit through another stupid assembly and watch another lame video to fix a problem I *knew* didn't exist.

It's not like when Memaw was a kid. She told me once that at her assemblies they got to watch cool movies like *You Can Pick Your Friends, but Please Don't Pick Your Nose* and *These Are Blasting Caps. Do Not Play with Them.*

I didn't know what blasting caps were, but they sound like way more fun than . . .

"That was really lame," I said.

Karl said, "Wow. Bully Boy looks a lot like—"

"What?" I said as we were both drowned out by the cheerleaders.

Then Phil wished everyone a bully-free day and the assembly was over.

Karl and I started back to class. Just as we stepped out of the cafetorium, we found Molly waiting for us.

She looked at me. "Are you okay?"

"Yeah, why?" I said.

"You know I was just teasing you the other day, right? I had no idea this could happen again."

"I'm fine. It's no big deal."

"What do you mean? Somebody stuffed you in a trash can and pushed you down the stairs. It's a huge deal!"

"Actually, Karl *kicked* me down the stairs."

Karl shrugged. "I thought he was a mummy."

"Wrapped in TP?" I said.

"I ate a bad Tot! Everyone knows they go straight to your brain!"

Molly rolled her eyes. "Whatever. The point is, we need to find who did this and—"

"What have you done?"

Molly's eyes went wide as she slowly looked past me. Karl and I wheeled around and came face-to-face with . . .

Roy pointed to Bully Boy, still on-screen in the cafetorium. "You didn't have to."

"I thought it looked like Roy too!" said Karl.

I shook my head. "Not helping."

Molly stepped forward. "Nick didn't have anything to do with that!"

Roy pointed down the hall. "What about her?"

Molly, Karl, and I looked past Roy to a crowd of kids surrounding . . .

I said, "How does a new kid get so popular so fast?"

"I don't know and I don't care," said Roy. "Just make sure that new girl doesn't point the finger at me."

"I don't control her," I cried as I turned around to Molly and Karl. "Tell him I don't control—"

But they were gone.

That's when I heard Simone say, "If we work together, we can stop this bully and take back our school! *Oui?*"

As I looked back down the hall, I could see that the crowd around Simone had grown by two. I watched as Molly and Karl cheered, *"Oui!"* along with everyone else.

I felt a tap on my shoulder.

Great. Not only have I let loose a bully who doesn't exist, I've ticked off a retired bully who does. And now my best friends have gone over to the Princess of Darkness.

Suddenly, one of those crazy things Memaw's always saying made sense.

CHAPTER 12

Simone's idea to raise money to rat out the bully was just the beginning. Over the next few days, the ZT assembly inspired all sorts of dumb campaigns.

There were Text-a-Bully posters all over school.

The OMGs passed out spray bottles of Mark-a-Bully (made from 100 percent pureed Jell-O-Meat).

SEE A BULLY
STOP A BULLY

TEXT: 5555

REMEMBER...
JELL-O-MEAT STAINS!

And the annoying girls from the Peer Mediation Club were EVERYWHERE!

Suddenly, normal stuff was seen as bullying. You couldn't tease a friend without a bunch of kids tattle-texting.

They were wrong.

You can bully yourself.

CHAPTER 13

Now that I had fake-bullied myself and brought ZT down on the school, everyone had their nose out of joint to do something. I discovered the "everyone" also included the Safety Patrol.

And after school I found out that the Safety Patrol now included Simone.

"What's she doing here?" I asked.

"I said she could help," said Molly.

"She doesn't belong in the Safety Patrol."

WE SHOULD HAVE A RAT-A-BULLY BAKE SALE TO RAISE MONEY FOR A REWARD.

I'LL MAKE TARTS!

TARTS?

"I'm the captain and I say she does."

"She hasn't been trained. She hasn't been bullied. She's not"—I leaned toward Molly and whispered—"one of us."

SHE'S NEW...

...SHE'S FRENCH...

...AND SHE'S IN!

"She makes a strong argument," said Karl as he rubbed his wrist.

Simone started to leave. "It is okay. I can tell when I am not welcome."

"That's not what I meant," I said.

"The three of you didn't belong anywhere until you belonged in Safety Patrol," said Mr. Dupree behind us.

We all turned around. Mr. Dupree was sitting on a bucket, wearing his pith helmet again. Like he'd been there the whole time. I swear he's a ninja.

Mr. Dupree continued, "Without Safety Patrol—"

"We'd probably be in Kid Protection and relocated to Guam," said Karl. "Like *that* kid at *that* school in his NanoNerd boxer-briefs, running down the hall from a bunch of scorpions that got loose after he dumped the sand from their terrarium into a flaming trash can where he'd put the pants he'd set on fire burning hydrogen gas from magnesium dissolved in acid!"

"That's not what happened," said Molly. "It was a world history class, and the kid was using a hot plate to make prehistoric bread. He set his shirt

on fire, tore it off, and threw it at the teacher, setting her wig on fire. The kid grabbed the wig and started stomping on it as everyone stared at the birthmark in the shape of Texas on his stomach."

"No. No. Except for the relocating to Guam, that's not even close to what happened," I said. "What I saw online was—"

"This is urban myth," said Simone. "In France, we hear it too. Sometimes principal's shirt is on fire. Sometimes it is teacher's wig. One time it was pet ferret in backpack. None of them ever happened."

"But I read it online," I said.

"I saw a squid tap-dance with a cat once on YouTube," said Karl.

Simone looked at me. "Everything you see on the Web, this you believe?"

I decided not to answer.

Mr. Dupree rolled his eyes. "If Safety Patrol is big enough for you three, it's big enough for Simone."

"But . . ." I said.

"But what?" asked Mr. Dupree.

But *everything*! Simone wasn't one of us. How many lockers had she been stuffed in? How many times had she been hung up by her shorts? How many times had she been described as freakishly tall? Or short? Or weird?

But I didn't say any of that. All I said was, "Nothing."

"Good," said Mr. Dupree. "So, what's up?"

Molly said, "I called this meeting to figure out

the best way to find who bullied Nick."

Simone looked at me. "You did not see who it is that bullied you?"

"I was wrapped in TP. I couldn't see anything."

Molly eyed me. "Yeah, about that . . . how could the bully use school TP? It only comes out one flimsy sheet at a time."

I shrugged. "I don't know. Maybe the bully brought some from home."

"Maybe the bully is this Emily," said Simone. "Maybe she has, how you say, a too-soft butt?"

Molly and Karl giggled.

"It wasn't Emily," I said.

"How can you be sure?" said Simone.

"Because Emily isn't a bully," I said. "I mean,

she wouldn't be a bully. I mean, if she's, you know, real."

"I thought you were sure Emily was real," said Mr. Duprce.

I looked down. "After today, I'm not so sure anymore."

When I looked back up, Simone was studying me. I imagined her trying to connect the dots—dots that would create a picture *nobody* needed to see.

I had to find a way to distract her from discovering the truth. I needed her to think I was the furthest thing from a bully.

"I wonder if Emily would be behind Zero Tolerance?" asked Karl.

Wait! That's it!

"Emily would love ZT!" I said. "She'd be totally behind it! Just like me!"

"You didn't look like you were behind ZT at the assembly," said Molly.

"You were not cheering," added Simone.

"I was cheering," I lied. "On the inside."

"I do that sometimes," said Karl. "It tickles."

I said, "We need to find the real bully. ZT is a good start. But what we need is to MEGASIZE ZERO TOLERANCE!"

Karl raised his hand. "My mom won't let me megasize anymore."

Simone nodded. "Yes, I like this idea. We should megasize a Rat-a-Bully bake sale. Raise more money for a bigger reward, *oui*?"

"That's good," I said. "But what if we went further? What if we questioned every student about where they were that morning?"

"And take everyone's phone to screen their texts," added Simone.

I nodded. "Don't forget lie detectors."

Simone's eyes went wide. "Twenty-four-hour video surveillance!"

"Good," I said, just before I went slightly over the top.

Everyone stared at me.

"Okay," I said. "No Dumpster Cat Pit of Terror. But we should do all we can. No kid deserves to be bullied. No exceptions!"

"'Let every eye negotiate for itself,'" said Mr. Dupree. "'And trust no agent; for beauty is a witch. Against whose charms faith melteth in blood.'"

"What?" said Simone.

"He's quoting Shakespeare," said Molly. "It's his thing. Just go with it."

I knew what was coming next:

"Did I ever tell you the story of my friend the worm farmer?"

"Now, THAT'S what I want to be when I grow up!" shouted Karl.

Mr. Dupree continued, "Birds were eating the farmer's worms, so he declared zero tolerance on birds."

We all shrugged.

"He declared zero tolerance on worms," said Mr. Dupree.

Karl raised his hand, "And the birds ate all the worms?"

CHAPTER 14

Just like with Memaw, I'm never quite sure what Mr. Dupree is trying to say. It must be some sort of grown-up thing. After school, I asked Becky what she thought.

"He's saying ZT *doesn't* work," said Becky. "If ZT had been around a few weeks ago, you and Roy would have both been suspended."

"This is different," I said.

"It's not different!"

She was right. But it didn't matter. I had already strapped myself to the ZT express.

I said, "You don't know what it's like to be picked on."

"I know what it's like," said Becky as she popped a piece of gum (she snuck it by her mom) into her mouth.

I looked down at my shoes and thought of pie until my stomach settled and I could continue.

"No, you really don't."

"Yes, I do."

"What, then?"

"It's embarrassing."

Maybe I wasn't the only one grossed out by her *gumnastics*.

"Tell me," I said.

Becky stopped chewing her gum. She whispered, "I can't do a cartwheel."

I laughed.

"It's not funny!"

"It's a little funny."

"When I tried out for cheerleader, I couldn't do a cartwheel. The other girls called me a freak and told me to go back to my beauty pageants."

"You were in—?"

"NO!" she yelled. "Well, once. My mom made me. It was horrible."

I bet she killed at the talent portion.

SPELLED HER NAME IN GUM

"Did you win?"

"Yes. BUT THAT'S NOT THE POINT! Now everyone thinks I'm this pageant princess, but I'm not. I get teased and picked on and just want to be normal like everyone else."

"Normal? You mean, like, *not* pretty."

"Sometimes."

I smiled. "So you're really not perfect."

Becky stared at me. "I can't do a cartwheel. I chew my hair. I grind my teeth."

"And you play with your gum," I added without thinking.

"What's up with that?"

"Wait. No. I'm sorry, I—"

"No," she said pointing to the sidewalk. "What's up with *that*?"

I said, "That's the Bully Watch—I mean, the thing we think is the Bully Watch symbol—inside a . . . guillotine?"

Becky looked at me. "A guillotine is French! Emily is warning is us about—"

"Simone?"

"What should we do?"

Time for a decision tree . . .

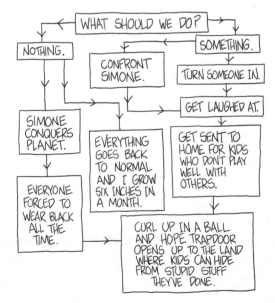

I shook my head. "It's not Emily. Someone's just messing with us."

"I thought you were sure Emily was real."

"I was, but . . . I don't know. Maybe it's like what Mr. Dupree said about the elephant. Maybe I was just seeing what I wanted to see."

Becky looked at me. "You really think all that Safety Patrol stuff with Roy was just coincidence? You really think these drawings don't mean anything?"

"Wow. You're really into this."

"I love a good mystery. And this is one I can really sink my teeth into," she said as she sank her teeth into a helpless wad of gum I swear I heard scream.

"I just have a hunch Simone is up something," said Becky. "She's gotten too popular too fast."

"Wait. You don't like Simone? I thought *everyone* liked Simone," I said.

"It's all that black she wears. It's just weird."

"I know. It's like, 'Look at me! I'm from France! I'm so cool! Watch me while I hypnotize your friends and steal them away!'"

"Steal your friends?"

"Simone is NOT a back-whacker!"

"What?"

"The other day I choked on a Tot. Molly whacked my back. She saved my life. Sort of."

"Sort of?"

"Okay, she did. Let's not get all weird about it. The point is, Molly's a back-whacker. She's my friend. Simone? I don't know what Simone is."

I'LL ALWAYS WHACK YOUR BACK.

THANKS.

"I gotta go," said Becky. "I'll see you tomorrow. And I'm going to keep an eye on Simone even if you won't."

"Whatever," I said.

As Becky walked off, I watched her twirl her gum between her fingers and her tongue like she was knitting a sweater. My stomach started to whine. Then it stopped. Maybe I was getting used to it. Maybe a little gross stuff isn't so bad if the person doing the gross stuff is kind of cool.

Then Becky started twirling the gum like a rope

in front of her face. She got too close and I watched as she whipped it right into her ear.

My stomach was quiet no more.

CHAPTER 15

That night, Phil came over for dinner again. Mr. Perfect brought Memaw macaroni-and-cheese tacos.

Memaw gave Phil her famous chocolate-chip cookies in return.

Memaw only gives cookies to people she really likes or really wants something from. Like when she wants half off on macaroni-and-cheese-flavored pretzels from the store manager at the Stop-N-Snarf.

It was starting to look like Memaw might tackle Phil and lock him in the basement for herself. I would have warned him, but I still wasn't a fan. Not that I've rooted for any of the other guys Mom's dated since she and Dad got divorced.

There have only been three guys other than Phil. Even though they were all different, they shared one thing in common: none of them was from this planet.

There was Big Dan, who wasn't all that big, 'cause he'd lost a lot of weight on some caveman diet.

BACON. ALL YOU NEED IS BACON. BACON. BACON AND MAYONNAISE. EAT ALL THE BACON AND MAYONNAISE YOU WANT. TRY SOME.

NO THANKS.

There was Ernie. Ernie was born without an upper lip. He was a lawyer.

He also thought he was a biker.

Ernie was not a biker.

There was Travis. Travis was a musician. He was very romantic. He once serenaded my mom outside her window at 2 a.m. on a Tuesday.

Unfortunately, Mom sleeps with earplugs, 'cause she has to get up for her 5 a.m. nursing shift at the emergency room.

The neighborhood dogs became big fans, though.

Now there's Perfect Phil, with his perfect hair and his perfect job and his perfect answers for questions about everything. Like how ketchup is made, and the history of socks, and why Emily Dickinson Middle School needs Zero Tolerance.

"Zero Tolerance works through deterrence," said Phil. "If a bully knows there are no exceptions, then it's just not worth it."

"But what if I'm bullied and then I bully back, but only I get caught. That wouldn't be fair."

Phil nodded. "It is unfair. And because it's so unfair, everyone will go out of their way to avoid bullying, because they don't want there to be any UNFAIR chance they'll get in trouble."

Memaw and Mom didn't say anything. I scratched my head. None of this made any sense at all. It must be another grown-up thing. They

must all be required to take adult continuing
education classes in confusing kids.

Memaw shook her head. "Phil, I like you and
I really like this mac-n-cheese taco, but what
you're describing sounds more like a jail than a
school."

"I'm sure Nick thinks it's already a jail," said
Phil, followed by an I'm-only-kidding-but-not-
really laugh.

Then he turned serious and leveled his
perfect eyes at Mom. "But it's really a school. For
learning. Kids can't learn if they spend all their
time worrying about being bullied."

Mom shook her head. "Of course not."

Phil shifted back to perfectly pleasant mode.
"And that's exactly why the board entrusted me
to run ZT. It helps me help make schools safe."

Phil smiled at me. "Don't you want to go to a safe school, Nick?"

Mom put her hand on my shoulder. "Aren't you tired of being bullied?

CHAPTER 16

"J*'accuse*," said Becky.

"Huh?" I said.

It was the next day and we were sitting outside before school, prepping for my French quiz.

"*J'accuse*," she said again. "This one's easy. It's just like it sounds."

"It is?" I asked as I watched Molly, Karl, and Simone set up their Rat-a-Bully bake sale across the schoolyard.

"Accuse," said Becky. "Like, 'I accuse you of a crime.'"

106

I tried, but I was too distracted by the circus going on across from us. In addition to the bake sale, the OMGs were handing out bottles of their guaranteed-to-stain Mark-a-Bully. Even the FIAs had gotten in on the action, selling handmade T-shirts.

The whole school was going nuts. And it was all MY fault. I started thinking about what everyone would do to me if they found out.

"Let's try another one," said Becky. *"Déjà vu?"*
"Déjà who?" I said.

"C'mon, Nick, focus!"

"Already seen?"

"Right! And it means?"

I shook my head.

"Remember? It's the feeling that you're reliving a moment you've lived before."

Déjà vu should have been easy to remember. All I had to do was look at my current mess, and instantly all my past messes would pop into my head.

"Have a tart!"

I looked up. It was Karl, holding a tray of tiny pies in front of us. Becky and I each tasted one.

"Wow!" said Becky. "This is incredible."

"Who made these?" I asked.

"I did," said Karl.

They were good. Scary good. Made me wonder what other hidden talents Karl had.

MAGIC?   JUGGLING?   SYNCHRONIZED SWIMMING?

Karl nodded to the crowd surrounding the bake sale. "Everyone seems to like them."

It was true. Both kids and teachers were buying. They were raising so much money they could pay someone to pretend to be the bully. I mean, other than me. Since, you know, I'd already shown I'd do it for free.

Becky and I walked over as Simone counted the take.

"Two hundred and twenty-two dollars!" she said. "And we're just getting started."

"Isn't that more than enough?" asked Becky.

Simone shook her head. "No one is going to

turn in a close friend for this. It has got to be more. *TRÈS* more!"

"Is paying kids to rat on each other really such a good idea?" I asked.

"What happened to Mr. No-One-Deserves-to-Be-Bullied?" asked Molly.

I knew where he was. He was up to his chin in quicksand.

Simone caught me eyeing the stack of cash in her hand. "You have a problem?" she said.

"It's just . . . you know, a lot of money."

Simone handed Molly the stack of cash. "That's why Molly is going to hold it."

Molly said, "No. You can keep it."

Simone said, "No. It is clear Nick does not trust me."

"That's not true," I lied. "There's no reason I wouldn't trust you."

Simone counted off with her fingers. "I am new. I am different. And I am, how you say? Shove-y?"

I nodded. "Pushy."

As Molly took the money from Simone, she glared at me. "Happy?" she said.

No. Not really.

CHAPTER 17

Madame Alamode was giddy as she handed me my quiz paper. "You were the only one in the whole class who got *déjà vu* correct," she said.

"Congratulations," said a voice from the hall.

I turned to see Molly standing at the classroom door.

"Hey," I said as I walked toward her.

She said, "You've been acting weird."

"Weird?"

"I mean, you know . . . more weird than usual."

"Um . . . thanks."

We started walking down the hall.

"Is it Simone?"

"No. Why would you think that?"

"Because you look at her like she's an alien sent to body-snatch me."

I shrugged. "She's okay."

"You know she's trying to help find who bullied you."

"I guess."

Molly stopped. Out of the corner of my eye, I thought I saw someone duck around a corner.

"You know, I can be friends with more than one person at a time. "

"I know."

"Give her a chance. She's not that bad."

I looked back down the hall. There was no one.

I looked back at Molly. Usually she looks at me like I'm an annoying puppy that keeps drinking out of the toilet until it falls in and has to be rescued from drowning. Like she wants to drop-kick me across the room, but she can't, because I'm so goofy and adorable.

But today she looked at me like a friend asking

for a favor. And it was for more than just payback for sort of saving me from choking to death. She wanted it because she . . . *really* wanted it.

I said. "Okay. Sure. I'll give Simone a chance."

We continued down the hall, pushed through the front doors, and walked outside.

"Becky seems nice."

"Yeah. Well . . ."

"Well what?"

"Nothing."

"Now you've got to tell me."

"She does this thing with her—"

"Gum? I KNOW!"

"IT'S DISGUSTING!" we both said at the same time.

I laughed. Molly laughed. Good times.

"I better go," said Molly. "Bye."

"Yeah, bye."

"What were you guys talking about?"

I turned around. It was Becky, standing right behind me. "Nothing," I said.

Becky looked down. "Uh-oh."

"What? We weren't talking about . . ."

Becky pointed to the sidewalk in front of us. "What's that?"

Right below us was another drawing.

"There's something else in the guillotine?" I said.
"Is that a . . . cake?"

"A really tiny one. Wait—it's a tart. Like the ones Karl makes."

Becky looked at me. "I don't get it."

I didn't get it either.

Becky stared at the sidewalk. "Bake sale? How would Simone kill a bake sale?"

I had no idea.

"It doesn't make any sense," I said.

"It has to mean Simone is up to something. We should tell someone."

"Tell them what? That some superkid or a ghost or a zombie that only you, Karl, and I think *might* be real drew some secret coded picture that *might* mean that the person trying their hardest to *find* my bully is about to *maybe* do something we can't figure out?"

Becky shook her head. "Well, not like *that*."

CHAPTER 18

Sometimes I talk to myself. I say stuff like, *Leave well enough alone. Don't get involved. Stop trying to hard-boil an egg in the microwave.*

The problem with talking to myself is that it's hard to talk and hear myself at the same time. Which is exactly what happened the next day, when I met Becky after school.

"Remember when I told you I was going to keep an eye on Simone?"

"What did you do?"

Becky showed me her phone. "See for yourself."

"Why is Karl wearing a beret?" I asked.

"It's not important," she said as another stick of gum flew into her mouth. "What *is* important is that Simone seems normal."

I stared at the pictures. "No. She's a lot more than normal. She's popular!"

As I handed Becky back her phone, I spotted Simone behind her saying good-bye to Molly and Karl. After they walked off, Simone turned and rushed back into the school.

"What's she doing?" I said.

Becky turned around. "She? You mean Simone?"

I don't know why I listened, but a feeling in my gut told me to chase after her.

I followed Simone to Molly's locker. She opened it, looked both ways down the hall, reached in and pulled out an . . . envelope!

That's when I knew the sidewalk drawing really was a warning. Simone was going to kill the bake sale by stealing the money!

The drawings really were by Emily! She was really REAL!

But I still needed proof, so I started taking pictures.

The pictures might be enough to get her into trouble, but they weren't enough for me. I needed her to know I'd caught her in the act.

That's when I realized that when you leap to conclusions, it's a good idea to have a firm landing area.

I did not have a firm landing area.

Together, we slid into the science lab and headed straight for . . .

But just as we were going to crash, we hit
dry floor and skidded to a stop, barely bumping
Charlie. I thought we were safe . . . until I
watched Charlie slide into the mouse cage. . .

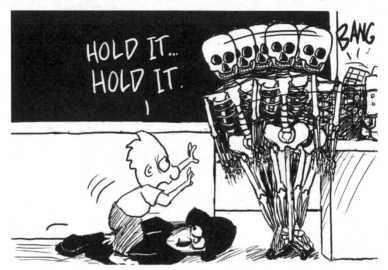

. . . knocking it over, scaring the mouse,

and, well . . .

. . . ruining my life.

I looked back to see Phil, Dr. Daniels, and Mr. Dupree all staring at me from the doorway.

"Nick attacked me!" yelled Simone.

I waved my phone. "She stole money! I have proof!"

That's when Becky, Molly, and Karl arrived.

"What are you all doing here?" I said.

Becky said, "I thought you might need help and got Karl and Molly to come too."

Molly stared at me. "He needs help, all right!"

I pointed at Simone. "She stole the bake sale money!"

Molly's eyes narrowed. "I TOLD HER TO GO BACK FOR IT!"

"He has hated on me since first I got here,"

said Simone. "He does not want me to make friends. He does not want me in Safety Patrol. He thinks *I* am a thief!" She pointed at me and yelled, "When *he* is THE BULLY!"

"I am not!" I protested. "I mean, I'm not *the* bully. Or *a* bully. I can explain! I . . . I . . ."

Perfect Phil pushed his perfect hand through his perfect hair while shaking his perfect head. "Nick, we saw you threatening Simone."

That's when I noticed Charlie's head still in my hands. "Oh . . . I mean, NO! It wasn't like that. I mean . . . the skeleton . . . was falling . . . after we bumped it. I slipped . . . when I jumped at her . . . because my gut said . . ."

Phil shook his head. "I'm sorry, Nick. Zero Tolerance means Zero Tolerance. I have no choice."

"No! No! You have choices! You have lots of choices. You can say it wasn't my fault. It was bad Tots! They go straight to your brain. That's it! I'm not guilty by reason of TEMPORARY BAD TOT INSANITY!"

Phil shook his head. "Nick, you're suspended."

CHAPTER 19

I've spent a lot of time in my room. It's not bad.
There's stuff to do. There are comic books to read,
video games to play, homework to ignore.

My room was fun back when . . . I COULD
LEAVE ANY TIME I WANTED!

Now that I'm suspended for three weeks and
grounded, my room feels like the Pit of Praxis.
The one with the Acid-Spitting Zombie Bats from
NanoNerd #87: "No Escape from Doom."

The worst part? I couldn't go on the field trip to King Potatamus's Egyptopolis (and Water Park), even though I'd gotten my grades up and learned how to say all sorts of useful stuff in French.

QU'EST CE QUI NE VA PAS AVEC MOI?*

* WHAT IS WRONG WITH ME?

I would have contacted the Kid Protection Program about relocating to Guam if Mom hadn't taken away my phone and computer.

"Nick isn't a bully."

"Um . . . he *was* sitting on top of Simone, threatening her with a skull."

Mom and Phil were talking in the hallway. I moved closer to listen.

"I'm sure he was just keeping it from hitting her," said Mom.

Go, Mom!

"He accused Simone of stealing money," said Phil.

Hmm . . . yeah . . . I did do that.

"Maybe he had a good reason," said Mom.

I did. Sort of.

"It wouldn't make a difference. Under Zero Tolerance, there's no room for appeal."

"It would make a difference to *me*," said Mom.

Hmm . . . should I tell her what really happened? I had to think about that.

I decided to come clean.

I opened the door. "What really happened was—"

"I got a text!" yelled Memaw, running toward us down the hall. "Someone texted me a picture. I think it has something to do with Nick."

Memaw showed me her phone.

It was Simone! She was the sidewalk artist! And the message was from . . . MLE? Emily?! Whoa. She really, *really* is real!

"Do you know that girl?" asked Mom. "And why is she drawing on the sidewalk?"

They say the truth can set you free. But I know better. I shrugged.

"That's the new girl," said Phil. "The one from France. The one Nick bullied."

Memaw looked at me. "MLE? What does that mean?"

I shrugged again.

"There's no rule against sidewalk drawings," said Phil. "Now, what were you going to tell us when Memaw ran up?"

Uh-oh. Three shrugs is pushing it. Time for another decision tree.

"Nothing," I said.

CHAPTER 20

Operation French Toast was operational. Or under way. Or in session. Or something.

Phase One: snatch Memaw's phone out of her purse so I could text for help.

I waited until I was sure Memaw and Mom were asleep before I snuck out of my room and tiptoed downstairs.

I found Memaw's purse. Unfortunately, I also found Memaw.

I had to find a way to move her hand without waking her.

You really don't want to startle Memaw awake. She sometimes freaks out.

I needed to distract her. But how?

囗入的祖丹 *

*ENTER THE GRANNY

FLOBT

I turned around to see our fart-terrier, Janice, smiling up at me. A second later the toxic cloud hit me.

After I ducked down in search of

PANT PANT PANT

MORPH-HORF-PHLOGORK...

oxygen, it hit me—a strategically placed Janice-bomb just might be enough to get Memaw to move her hand without waking her.

I quietly led Janice to the middle of the living room. "Lie down," I whispered.

Janice lay down while I ducked and covered behind a chair. "Fart," I commanded.

I waited. Memaw didn't move.

I slid Janice closer, hid again, and whispered, "Fart!"

YES! I grabbed the purse, snatched Memaw's phone, and beat it back to my room. Phase One of Operation French Toast was now complete. Now it was time for Phase Two: text for reinforcements.

I sent Becky the picture of Simone drawing on the sidewalk.

Nick: It's Nick on Memaw's phone. U send this?

Becky: No. OMG! Simone is copycatting Emily! She set U up!

Nick: She's toast. French toast.

Becky: Not that funny.

Nick: A little funny.

Becky: What r u going to do?

Nick: Grounded. Got plan. Need help. Need u to keep i on Simone.

Becky: Will try.

Nick: Thanks. Later.

Becky: Potater.

Nick: Really not that funny.

Becky: Shut up.

Becky was a good start, but I needed somebody on the inside. I needed somebody in Safety Patrol who was close to Simone and wasn't Molly. That meant only one person:

WEARS A BERET

AFRAID OF HEIGHTS →

AFRAID OF → MUMMIES

WANTS TO BE A WORM FARMER →

AFRAID OF COSTUMED CHARACTERS

TELLS YOU WAY MORE THAN YOU WANT TO KNOW ABOUT ← SLOTHS.

I might be in trouble.

I texted the picture of Simone to Karl:

Nick: It's Nick on Memaw's phone. Need ur help.

Karl: I'm a good helper.

Nick: Right. See the picture.

Karl: Is that Simone?

Nick: She drew the picture. She set me up!

Karl: She set me up too. With a beret!

Nick: No. She set me up 2 get caught.

Karl: Simone is pretending to b Emily?

Nick: Yes!

Karl: HOW RUDE!

Nick: U help me?

Karl: Can I keep the beret?

Nick: Yes. Keep the beret.

Karl: !!!!!!!

Nick: Great. I need u 2 b my eyes and ears at school.

Karl: Oo! Oo! I know how!

Nick: Save it for 2morrow nite at my place.

Karl: It's a really good idea.

Nick: Great. Good nite.

Karl: Don't let the sea monkeys bite.

Nick: Say good nite, Karl.

Karl: Good nite, Karl.

CHAPTER 21

The next afternoon I heard Becky and Karl whispering outside my window.

"Just tap on the window."

"But how will he know it's us?"

"Who else would it be?"

"We could be anybody. We could be zombies or aliens or terrierists."

"You mean terrorists."

136

I threw open the window. "Get in here now!"

"See? He knew it was us," said Becky.

Karl shook his head. "This time."

Becky crawled in, followed by Karl, dragging his suitcase backpack. They each took a seat on my bed. Becky immediately unwrapped a stick of gum, and my stomach started whining.

"So, why did Simone set you up?" asked Becky.

Karl raised his hand. "Oo! Oo! I know!"

"What, Karl?" I said.

"She hates you."

"But why?" asked Becky.

Karl raised his hand again. "Oo! Oo!

I said, "You don't have to raise your hand, Karl."

Karl said, "Because Nick doesn't like her."

"So? I don't like most kids," I said. "And none of them has ever tried to get me kicked out of school."

"Maybe she wants you kicked out for some other reason," said Becky.

"Like what?" I said.

"What if Simone wants you kicked out of school so she can be friends with Molly herself?" asked Karl.

Molly and I stared at him.

"What?" said Karl. "I didn't raise my hand."

Becky nodded. "No. That actually makes sense."

Karl pumped his fist. "Yes!"

"Wait," I said. "When Molly and I were talking the other day, I saw someone watching us down the hall. What if it was Simone?"

"But that would mean Simone wanted you and Molly to continue to be friends," said Becky.

"That's it!" I said. "Simone wanted Molly to think I was cool with them being friends so that when I went after Simone, Molly would think I'd lied to her."

Becky nodded. "That's like serious next-level mean-girl stuff."

Karl raised his hand again. "Is everyone from France an evil genius?"

I ignored him. "So Simone set this whole thing up to get rid of me and make Molly think I'm a rat. Now we have to figure out a way to expose Simone for who she really is."

"How?" asked Becky.

Karl stood up.

KARL TO THE RESCUE!

"Rescue?" I said.

Karl unzipped his suitcase backpack and started taking out a baby monitor and some other electronic stuff.

I said, "What's all this?"

...YOUR EYES AND EARS!

IT'S A BERET-CAM WITH A MICROPHONE INSIDE.

IT TRANSMITS TO A SECURE WEB SITE THROUGH MY FANNY PACK. I CAN HEAR THROUGH A HIDDEN EAR BUD.

AND YOU CAN WATCH **LIVE** ON THIS BABY MONITOR!

I said, "This is great, Karl!"

"My mom was using it to find out if my dad was getting up in the middle of the night to sneak pickles," explained Karl.

"Isn't she going to notice it's gone?" asked Becky.

"No," said Karl. "Because when my dad found the cam, he dropped it in the pickle jar."

"But it still works?" I asked.

"It smells a little garlicky, but yeah."

"Way to go, Karl!" cried Becky.

Karl rocked back and forth on his heels and smiled.

"This is my very first plan! Can I let Stanley know?"

"Um . . . sure. Okay," I said.

"OHMYGAWD!" cried Karl. "Stanley pooped. In front of people! For the first time! He must REALLY like you two!"

CHAPTER 22

Karl's Beret-Cam worked like a charm. I could see everything Karl could see. Which, due to Karl's very shy and very small bladder, was a LOT of the boys' bathroom.

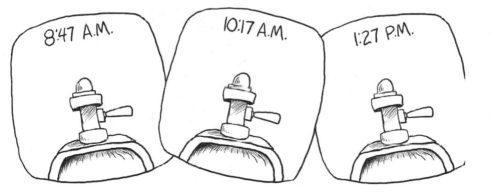

8:47 A.M.   10:17 A.M.   1:27 P.M.

When Karl wasn't in the bathroom, I could see Simone had become more popular since I'd been suspended.

The OMGs were now under her spell.

Roy and the FIAs were totally on board.

Everyone was so eager to get on the Simone bandwagon that the Safety Patrol Rat-a-Bully bake sale had now raised over $500.

As I watched, I realized . . .

By the end of the school day, I was still no closer to exposing Simone. I was about to give up when the Beret-Cam spotted her getting a call at her locker. She checked the caller ID but didn't answer. Then she slammed her locker shut and took off down the hall.

"Follow her!" I yelled into Karl's earpiece.

The Beret-Cam shook as Karl jogged after Simone.

"But I have to pee," said Karl.

"Again?"

"You know I have a—"

"Just hold it!"

Karl rounded a corner just in time to catch Simone heading into the girls' locker room.

He stopped.

"Keep going," I said.

"I can't!"

"Do it!"

Karl took the Beret-Cam off and turned it on himself.

"You won't go blind," I calmly explained. "It's after school. The girls' soccer team is out practicing. The locker room is empty."

"I won't do it. You can't make me."

"If you do this, I'll sit next to you at lunch for the rest of the school year."

"Across from or next to?"

"Across from."

There was a long pause.

"Okay. Next to," I said.

"And I get all your Tots."

"Fine!"

This better be worth it, I thought.

Karl entered the girls' locker room. Simone was nowhere in sight. Karl stopped at a pile of folded towels. He picked one up and smelled it.

Karl whispered, "Why do the girls get fabric softener and we don't?"

"Focus!" I hissed.

Karl moved deeper into the locker room. I could hear Simone's voice in the distance, but I couldn't make out what she was saying.

"Get closer," I said.

"How?"

"See that hamper over there? Get in, cover yourself with some towels, and slide yourself closer."

Karl approached the hamper. I watched as he picked up one of the towels from inside and sniffed.

"These are nasty. There's no way—"

"GET! IN! OR NO TOTS!"

Karl grunted and climbed in. He covered himself in towels and the screen went dark. Then I heard an "omph!" as he pushed off of a locker. I could hear the cart rolling when . . .

✧CRASH✧

I held my breath. A few seconds passed. Finally, Simone started talking again.

"Mom, you've got to stop calling all the time!" she said. "I'm fine. No one here has any idea what happened before."

"She sounds weird," whispered Karl.

Karl was right. There was something strange about her voice. Then it hit me. Her French accent was GONE!

She said, "No! Please don't. You really don't need to talk to the guidance counselor. Besides, you promised me you'd stay out of it."

"I don't think she's really French," whispered Karl.

"Shut up!" I hissed.

"Wait. Hang on," said Simone. There was a pause; then, loudly she asked, "Is someone there?"

After a few seconds, Simone said, "I gotta go, Mom. Bye."

I could hear Simone walking away. Karl lifted his head.

"Wait!" I said.

"No," he said. "The longer I'm in here, the more therapy I'll need later."

As Karl climbed out of the hamper, the Beret-Cam picked up something that looked exactly like . . .

"Simone's backpack!" I yelled. "Get down!"

Karl dived back into the hamper. The Beret-Cam didn't. I watched as it flew off Karl's head and landed on the floor.

"Karl, the beret!" I whisper-shouted.

But it was too late.

CHAPTER 23

Maybe they won't come down too hard on you," said Becky.

I stared at her.

"Sorry. It seemed like the thing to say."

It was later that afternoon. Becky and Karl had snuck back into my room.

Karl was freaking out. "I've never been suspended. I've never been in trouble. Now I have to repeat seventh grade or go into the Kid Protection Program and move to France to raise worms."

"Wait," said Becky. "Simone knows you two

spied on her, right? So now we know Simone's a phony and she knows that if she turns you in, *you* can turn *her* in."

Karl threw up his arms. "Great! Then everybody will move to France and raise worms. We'll flood the market!"

"No. Then it's a standoff," said Becky.

"Maybe," I said. "But a standoff doesn't help Molly. We still don't really know what Simone is up to. We don't know why she's pretending to be French. Or why she wants me expelled. Molly could be in real trouble. We've got to warn her!"

"Nick, can I come in?" called Memaw from the hallway.

"Just a second, Memaw!"

"Quick! Hide!" I whispered.

Becky ducked into my closet. Karl tried to follow, but it wasn't big enough for both of them.

"Are you decent?" asked Memaw.

"Um . . . hang on. I'm coming."

Karl wouldn't fit under the bed either. Or under the desk.

Memaw said, "You're not dressing up with your underwear around your neck like that Nerd Boy character again, are you?"

"It's NanoNerd! And it's a battle scarf!"
Becky giggled.

"Shut up!" I whispered.

"Every time you do that, it stretches them out," said Memaw.

"Just . . . WHATEVER! I'm almost there!"

The only place left for Karl to hide was my old toy chest. I dumped everything out and Karl climbed in. It was a tight fit.

Memaw walked in. "Once that elastic goes, the only place your tighty-whities will fit is around your ankles."

I smiled. "What's up?"

Memaw nodded toward the hallway. "Someone's here to see you."

That's when the last person I expected to see stepped into my room.

Memaw left us alone as Molly stared at the old toys scattered on the floor. "Wow. You must be really bored."

I shook my head. "No. Not really."

Molly took a deep breath. "I just came over to say . . . you know . . . I'm sorry you've been suspended."

"*You're* sorry?" I said.

"It's just that . . . I think it's my fault."

Wait—she's not mad. She doesn't know what happened. Which means Simone hasn't told her. Maybe Simone hasn't told anyone.

Molly said, "I didn't do a good job explaining the other day."

"You want to be friends with Simone. I get it."

She shook her head. "No. You don't. If you did, none of this would've happened."

Now was my chance to tell her the truth about Simone.

"Molly, Simone isn't—"

"—who you think she is," interrupted Molly. "Simone's great," she continued. "Girls have always been . . . I don't know . . . scared of me. I'm *freakishly* tall! But with Simone I feel . . . you know, normal.

"Anyway, what were you going to say?" asked Molly.

"Nothing."

There was no way I could tell her the truth about Simone.

I'd break her heart.

"Still friends?" she asked.

I nodded.

Molly started for the door. After a few steps she stopped and looked back. "You know, Simone feels really bad about what happened. She wanted me to tell you she's sorry."

"Wait. She knows you're here?"

"Yeah. It was her idea," said Molly. "See? She's not so bad. She just wants everyone to get along."

CHAPTER 24

After Molly left, I stood in the middle of my room and stared at my shoes.

Becky opened the closet door. "Why didn't you tell her about Simone?"

I shook my head. "She thinks she's all normal now. I can't take that away from her."

"But she's probably calling Simone right now. She's going to know you didn't rat her out. There'll be nothing to stop her from turning you in."

"I know."

Karl stuck his hand out of the toy chest. "A little help?"

"You're going to have to repeat seventh grade," said Becky.

I nodded. "Or pack for Guam."

"Wait. What if *I* turned her in?" said Becky.

"I'll turn her in too," added Karl. "Right after you get me out of here."

I shook my head. "No. I'll turn myself in. And I'll say it was all my idea. And I'll say it was me in the locker room so Karl won't get suspended."

"Thanks, but I'm sort of suspended right now. IN THIS BOX!" yelled Karl.

Becky and I said, "Oh," at the same moment as we rushed over to help.

"I think you should sit tight," said Becky. "We don't really know what Simone's going to do. We could have her all wrong."

"Maybe," I said, just as Karl's Beret-Cam on my desk flickered back on.

"But probably not."

CHAPTER 25

When you go to a school named after Emily Dickinson, they make you study stuff about her.

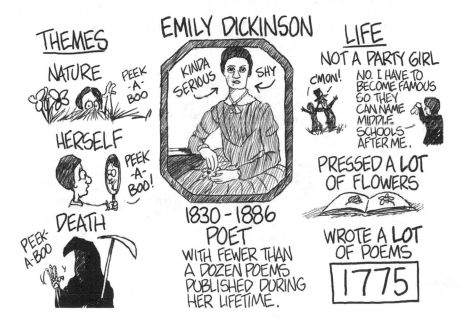

In English they make us memorize one of her poems. None of them made much sense to me. So

I picked the one that seemed the least boring. I think it started like this:

Because I could not stop for Death—
He kindly stopped for me—
The Carriage held but just Ourselves—
And Immortality.

As I lay on my bed, the poem suddenly made a lot more sense. At least it did after some rewriting:

Because I could not stop for Doom—
He kindly stopped for me.
His Doommobile held but just ourselves.
Next stop: Guam.

"Nick!" yelled Memaw from outside my door. "Come in."

Memaw entered. She looked worried. "I just got a call from your mom. She says the two of you are supposed to meet Phil down at school this afternoon."

"On a Saturday?"

Memaw eyed me. "What's going on?"

I shrugged.

Memaw shook her head. "Shrugging is for hiding ugly neck tattoos and for football players who forget their shoulder pads."

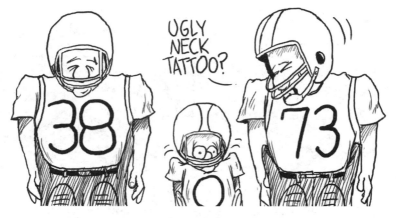

"I really don't know," I lied.

Memaw handed me her phone. "Would it have anything to do with *this*?"

It was another text message from MLE. I clicked on the link.

"That's Simone! SHE'S *that* kid from *that* school!" I cried.

"What kid from what school?" asked Memaw.

I quickly went over my options.

I told her everything.

When I finished, Memaw closed her eyes and smiled. "Your mom swears you were never dropped on your head. But you and I know better."

"It all makes sense now," I said. "Simone pretended to be French because she didn't want anyone to find out her secret. She must have thought I was on to her, so she set me up to bully her so I'd get kicked out of school."

Memaw took back her phone. "We need to tell Phil what's going on."

"No! We can't!"

"Why? Are you protecting somebody?"

"Maybe."

"Nick, I'm sure whoever it is will understand why you have to tell Phil about Simone."

I shook my head. "No, she won't."

Memaw looked me in the eye. "This is a friend?"

"She saved my life."

"What?"

"I was choking on a Tot."

Memaw sighed. "You understand that keeping your promise means you'll get expelled and have to repeat seventh grade?"

I looked down and nodded. "Why can't I just be normal?"

Memaw reached for me.

She let go and looked me in the eye. "Always remember, a normal chicken has one head. But a two-headed chicken is a lot more fun at parties."

Even though I had no idea what she was talking about, she somehow made me feel better.

"What if you talked to Simone?" asked Memaw.

"Why would she talk to me? She knows I won't reveal her secret."

Memaw looked at her phone. "There are worse

things than accidentally setting a principal's sleeve on fire. And exposing the principal's . . . What did you call that thing?"

"A Deathicorn."

"Mercy. Anyway, you've survived stuff just as bad without having to move to a new school."

"Not really."

"Said the kid about to repeat seventh grade."

"Okay. Maybe."

"It's settled, then. We'll talk to her before meeting with Phil."

"That's in three hours! I don't know where she is!"

"There must be some way we can find her. Who does she hang out with?"

"Molly. Sometimes Karl."

"What're they doing today?"

"They're at the . . . Wait! They're on the King Potatamus field trip!"

"Would Simone be there?"

"Everyone's there! I mean . . . except me."

"Let's go," said Memaw. "I'll drive."

"You?"

"What?"

"Nothing."

That's when I realized that the hardest part

of Memaw's plan wasn't going to be changing
Simone's mind. . . .

It was going to be getting to the park
sometime in my lifetime.

Memaw, the light changed."

"Are you sure?"

"I'm sure."

"You're *sure*?"

"I'M SURE!"

We had been stopped at an intersection through three green lights.

I looked out the rear window. A line of honking cars stretched behind us.

"You're sure it's not red?" asked Memaw.

"It's green," I said. "You need to go. Before—"

"You're sure it changed?"

"It's red again."

"Well, make up your mind!"

Memaw is red/green color-blind. I have no idea how she keeps her driver's license. I have a hunch it has something to do with cookies.

Memaw looked left and right. "Where is this Queen Hapless's Egypt World of Water?"

"Just ahead. And it's King Potatamus's Egyptopolis and Water Park."

"Is King Pantsless's Egyptian Wacky Planet the one with the hopscotch walrus?"

"Hip-hop hippo."

"Right. The one on the commercials."

"Please stop," I said.

"What? I got skills!"

I pointed. "The light's changed. Go!"

"You're sure?"

"DRIVE!"

Memaw moved forward at the speed of ketchup.

Fortunately, the park was only a couple of blocks ahead.

Memaw turned at the sign and slowly circled the massive parking lot. She eventually parked in a handicapped space in front of the entrance.

I said, "Memaw, you're not handicapped."

Memaw smiled as she hung her handmade handicapped sign.

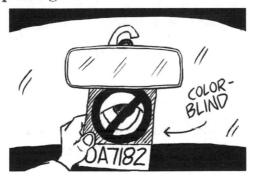

We got out of the car and approached the entrance.

"The park is closed for a private function," said a familiar voice behind us.

MR. DUPREE?   NICK?

"What are you doing here?" I asked.

"What are *you* doing here?" asked Mr. Dupree.

"Who is this handsome fellow?" asked Memaw.

"Handsome? What?"

Mr. Dupree smiled at Memaw. "I'm Sky Dupree."

"Sky?" I said out loud.

Mr. Dupree continued, "I'm the janitor at Nick's school and I also help out with Safety Patrol. On weekends I work security here at the park."

"Seriously? Sky?" I said.

Memaw stuck out her hand. "I'm Maxine, but all my gentleman callers call me Max."

"What gentleman callers?" I asked.

Memaw ignored me as they shook hands and did that creepy stare-at-each-other-not-saying-anything thing for way longer than was comfortable.

I had to interrupt. "You're a janitor *and* a water park cop?"

"'His acts being seven ages,'" added Memaw.

Mr. Dupree smiled. "A fan of the bard?"

Memaw nodded and smiled. Mr. Dupree smiled wider. And I threw up a little inside.

I interrupted again. "We have to find the field trip."

Mr. Dupree shook his head. "Nick, you know I can't let you in."

"It's an emergency!" I begged. "You don't understand, I have to . . . "

Memaw suddenly moved to Mr. Dupree's side. "'Yet I know the sound: Art thou not Romeo and a Montague?'"

I thought they'd lost their minds, until I noticed Memaw pointing to the entrance behind her back. She announced, "'The orchard walls are high and hard to climb.'"

The orchard walls? Wait . . . she means the entrance. She's trying to cover my escape. Cool!

I started tiptoeing away. "'For stony limits cannot hold love out,'" said Mr. Dupree.

As I slipped past the gate and started running, I heard Memaw yell, "'If they do see thee . . .

CHAPTER 27

From my hiding place behind a Ra the Sun God Recyclable Receptacle I watched a pimply-faced pharaoh wheel an overflowing trash bin toward the back of King Potatamus's Play Palace.

He disappeared around the corner and I made my move. I ran for the kitchen door as it was closing, slipped through, and dived under a counter.

I had a plan. Not my best plan. But under the circumstances, it was all I could come up with.

I obviously couldn't go through the front entrance without being recognized, so I figured I would somehow go through the kitchen, then somehow peek into the arcade, then somehow get Molly's, Karl's, or Becky's attention, then somehow get Simone to come to me, then somehow convince her that there are worse things than accidentally setting your principal's sleeve on fire.

That's a lot of *somehow*s. Too many *somehow*s.

But sometimes, when you're lucky, *somehow*s turn into *that's-how*s . . . like when King Potatamus himself (or at least the sweaty kid inside) burst through the kitchen door and ripped off his headpiece.

THOSE SNOTS SHOVED PIZZA THROUGH MY AIR VENT!

He tore off the rest of his costume, kicked it aside, and stormed into the kitchen bathroom.

I didn't hesitate. Even though the costume reeked of soda and pizza and was WAY too sticky

(What did he do? Eat in there?), I quickly put it on and stumbled into the arcade before I realized . . .

I was too short for the costume! The view screen was at least two feet above me. I was a blind hippo pharaoh in a room full of sugar-hyped kids armed with pizza. I was doomed!

Suddenly, I felt something hot and squishy slide into my costume.

"He-HEEEEE!"

I knew that laugh. It came from Norman Woogurt. Only Norman laughs like a chipmunk on helium.

I craned my neck and saw that he'd shoved a slice of pizza through the back ventilation screen. It was gross, but it was also great, because the screen was exactly at my eye level. When I turned myself around I could see and walk King Potatamus backward at the SAME TIME!

Everything was still going sort of according to plan!

But before I could look for Simone, I had to square things with Norman. Even as a temporarily costumed character, I was still honor bound to defend my costume. It's a law or something.

I grabbed what was left of the slice, marched backward up to Norman, stuck my arm out the screen, and shoved it down the back of his pants.

"Hey! You can't do that!" he cried.

"I just did!" I growled.

He slowly backed away. That's when all the enormous power that comes with being a costumed character washed over me.

Now that I'd brought down a world of hippo hurt on Norman, I could move forward—I mean, backward—with my plan.

I scanned the arcade for Simone. She wasn't under the monitor playing King Potatamus's latest music video.

She wasn't playing Whack-a-Sphinx or Tomb Invader.

Where was she?

"Stay back, you foul, water-dwelling beast!"

Karl? I turned to look and spotted him on the opposite side of the arcade, slowly backing away. "You can't have my soul!" he yelled.

I yelled back, "Karl! Wait! It's me, Nick!"

"Huh? Nick? Is that *you*?"

I turned. Becky was standing next to me.

"Um . . . yeah," I said.

"What are you doing here?" she asked as Karl fled to the bathroom. "And what's up with Karl?"

"I'm here to talk to Simone," I said. "And Karl's afraid of costumed characters."

"What? Wait. Why do you have to talk to Simone?"

I brought Becky up to speed.

"Simone is *that* kid at *that* school?" said Becky. "Wow! That's . . . Wow! That explains—"

"Everything."

"What are you going to say to her? I mean, what *can* you say to her?"

"After I find her I'll explain everything."

Becky pointed across the room. "She's right over there with Molly."

Simone was holding court near the stage, surrounded by every clique from school. In the middle of it all stood Molly.

But before I could move, an amplified voice blared, "Ladies and gentlemen! Boys and girls! Put your hands together for Queen Nefi and the Tuts!"

I looked past Simone to the stage as four animatronic mummies rose through openings in the floor. But something was wrong. As they rose, I remained level with them. I looked down through the screen.

I was perched on Queen Nefi's shoulders! I must have been standing on the spot where she rises out of the floor. As she rose, I rose with her. And we were still rising!

Since I was facing backward in the costume, there was no way I could get down. I watched helplessly as we rose higher and higher. That's when I remembered that Queen Nefi rises high above the stage to do her famous Mummy Dance. . . .

We kept rising. Just when I thought, How much higher can we go? King Potatamus's head hit the ceiling. But Queen Nefi didn't stop. She kept pushing me up from below.

I was just about to freak out when I thought, Wait! WWNND? What would NanoNerd do?

Not helpful.

Then, just as I was imagining what kids would say at my funeral . . .

CRUSHED IN A HIPPO COSTUME BY AN ANIMATRONIC EGYPTIAN HIP-HOP QUEEN.

WE ALL HAVE TO GO SOME TIME, BUT NO ONE SHOULD HAVE TO GO LIKE THAT.

. . . Queen Nefi stopped rising.

And started to dance.

Sort of.

WHIRRR

WHINE!

With the costume wedged between her and the ceiling, she could barely move. I could hear the motors inside Queen Nefi strain as one of her arms got pinned against Potatamus's leg. The whine grew louder and louder, until. . .

Queen Nefi fell, taking the costume—and my pants—with her.

"Nick?"

It was Perfect Phil with his Perfect Hair, standing at the edge of the gaping crowd of kids below. I

was impressed. He'd spent the morning and the early afternoon chaperoning the field trip while keeping the late afternoon open for destroying my life. He's quite the multitasker.

"Drop down!" he said. "I'll catch you."

I had a choice. I could endure the added

humiliation of having Perfect Phil perfectly catch me
or I could continue to hang there in my underwear
before the entire school. Before I could decide, my
lack of upper-body strength chose for me.

I landed on my back. When I opened my eyes,
Molly's face came into view. "Are you okay?"

"Yeah . . . I think so."

"What's going on? Why? I mean, how? I mean,
what are you doing here?" she asked.

Phil stepped up. "Nick, you know you're not
supposed to be here."

Molly looked down at my legs. "And where are
your pants?"

My pants?! I searched around me. No pants,
but I did find the bottom half of King Potatamus's
costume. I quickly pulled it back on.

As the laughter faded, I spotted Simone staring at me from behind Molly and Phil.

"I know what's going on," I said to Simone. "I just need to talk to you."

"Know what?" said Molly.

Molly turned to Simone as she slowly backed into the crowd. "What does Nick know?"

"I can't tell her," I yelled to Simone. "Only you can."

"What's going on?" asked Phil.

"Tell me WHAT?" cried Molly. "Will somebody please tell me WHAT'S GOING ON?"

"EVERYBODY, LEAVE ME ALONE!" yelled Simone from the front entrance.

Molly rushed toward Simone. "Wait!" she cried.

Simone pushed through the doors and was gone.

Becky turned to me. "I'll go after them."

As Becky took off, I yelled, "You can't tell her! Simone has to tell her!"

"Tell her what?" asked Phil.

"What do you care?"

A voice yelled, "Look out!"

I looked up.

Just as I thought things couldn't get any worse, I heard a familiar scream behind me.

I looked out through the screen. It was Karl. Armed with an oversize trash can. Aimed directly at me.

CHAPTER 28

When one of your friends has you trapped under an overturned trash can, you don't have a lot of options:

186

I was about to go the spit route when something strange and weird and very, very Emily happened.

I disappeared. Sort of.

"Let Nick go, Karl," said Phil.

"That's not Nick under there," said Karl.

I said, "It's me, Karl."

"Everyone knows costumed characters lie," Karl explained.

"Karl, step aside or go to detention," said Phil.

Karl stepped back. "It's *your* soul."

Before I could brace my hands for impact, the floor opened up under me.

I fell through and landed . . .

Unfortunately, no. I'd fallen through the trapdoor Queen Nefi came up through. Someone must have opened it. Someone like . . .

Above me, I heard a gasp from the crowd.

"What the . . . ? Where did he go?" said Phil.

"NOW does everyone believe me?" yelled Karl.

"The trapdoor!" cried Phil. "He's under the floor!"

I yanked off the headpiece and tried to look for a way out. I couldn't see a thing until . . .

I crawled toward the light and tumbled out a small maintenance door. It took a few seconds for my eyes to adjust and see . . . two adults staring down at me.

CHAPTER 29

Memaw said, "After I explained the Simone situation to Sky—"

I said, "Please stop calling him Sky."

She ignored me and continued, "We ran to the arcade and saw you were trapped. Sky released the trapdoor."

Mr. Dupree looked at me. "You're going to need to cover up."

I looked down and realized I was still missing my pants.

"Wrap yourself in this," said Memaw as she handed me a towel. "I swiped it when we saw you were pantsless."

Mr. Dupree said, "Both of you, follow me."

Mr. Dupree led Memaw and me to a door set inside a fake rock wall. The door opened onto a flight of stairs leading *under* the park.

Mr. Dupree started down the stairs. "Maxine explained everything. Come on, this is the fastest way to find Simone."

Memaw and I followed. The stairs led to a wide tunnel that stretched in both directions. Directly across was a door labeled SECURITY. Mr. Dupree opened the door . . . to the entire park!

"She's headed for the Flying Pyramid," said Mr. Dupree. "We just need to get ahead of her."

"But that's on the other side of the park!" I said.

"Not a problem," said Mr. Dupree.

He hit a switch on the side of the tunnel, and a large door slid open revealing . . .

"It's faster than it looks," said Mr. Dupree.

We climbed in. That's when I discovered that not all older drivers are like Memaw. A few, like Mr. Dupree, drive like they're being chased by Gafarbian Snow Eels (*NanoNerd* #73: "Snow Man Is an Island").

I don't remember much of what happened next, mostly because I tend to pass out when my body is subjected to anything over seven G's.

When we finally stopped, I opened my eyes to see Mr. Dupree standing at the foot of another stairway. "The Flying Pyramid is right above us."

We rushed up the stairs, out the back of a fake baobab tree, into the park, and stopped directly in front of . . .

Behind Simone, I could see Molly and Becky running to catch up.

"Simone!" cried Molly.

Simone turned to Molly, then back to me, and then to the Flying Pyramid.

She ran for the ride.

With Molly and me right behind her.

As we ran, I looked from the top of the Flying Pyramid to the zip line that spans the park.

I had never ridden the zip line, because I was never tall enough . . . until now. . . .

Molly continued after Simone as I stood frozen in place.

Becky ran up. "What are you doing? We have to go after them."

I tried to move, but I couldn't. I suddenly realized that sometimes it's okay to be the thing you hate when the thing you hate keeps you from doing the thing you're too scared to do.

Becky grabbed my arm. "Let's go!"

I didn't budge.

"Simone! Wait!" yelled Molly.

I looked up and watched Molly grab Simone's arm on the pyramid stairs.

"Leave me alone!" yelled Simone.

"Wait. Your voice. What happened to your accent?"

"I'm not French, dummy!"

"You're not . . . ?"

"I'm *that* kid from *that* school!"

"Wait. What?"

"The one who set—?"

"The principal on fire?!"

"It was his SLEEVE!"

"THE DEATHICORN TATTOO?"

"Still want to be friends?"

Molly let go of Simone's arm.

"I thought so," said Simone as she started back up the stairs.

"Wait!" said Molly.

Molly grabbed Simone's foot. After a few seconds of tug-of-war, Molly pulled hard at the same moment Simone yanked her foot forward.

Simone broke free and sprinted up the stairs, unaware that Molly had lost her footing behind her.

Molly fell.

And I ran.

Eventually.

CHAPTER 30

As Becky and I ran to the base of the stairs, I looked back. Mr. Dupree and Memaw were still a good distance away. Behind them, I spotted Phil leading the field-trip kids. He was closing fast.

We arrived at the stairs. I looked up. Molly was slumped against the railing a few flights up. She was rubbing her ankle but otherwise looked okay.

I turned to Becky. "I need you to stall while I go up after Molly and Simone."

"Stall? How?"

"I don't know. . . . Wait. Bring the crazy!"

"What?"

"Remember those times I went nuts in front of Roy in the cafetorium and during the fire drill?"

"I can't do that. I'm not like you. I'm—"

"Normal?"

"That's not what I was going to say."

"Normal? You torture gum and use it as jump rope. You constantly interrupt. And you think people don't know stuff when they do."

Wait. Did I just say that out loud?

"What are you talking about?" said Becky. "I don't do any of those—"

"Um . . . I'm sorry," I said. "It's just . . . you know, you're—"

"Different?" said Becky. "Wait. I just interrupted you, didn't I?"

"Uh-huh."

"Okay. Maybe I'm a little different. It's just that everyone thinks I'm this perfect princess, when I'm not. I just want to be like everyone else!"

I didn't say anything.

"That was one of those things I thought you didn't know that you do know, wasn't it?"

I nodded.

"Okay, maybe I'm a LOT different."

I started up the stairs. "Great! Use that when you bring the crazy!"

"I don't like you right now!" yelled Becky.

I smiled as I looked up ahead. I could see Molly. Past her, Simone continued climbing to the top.

I looked down. Memaw, Mr. Dupree, Phil, and the rest of the students were all staring at Becky as she brought her own special kind of crazy.

"Leave me alone!"

It was Molly, a couple flights above me. She was staring at her shoes and rubbing her ankle. I said, "Are you okay?"

Molly looked down at me with tears in her eyes. "Stop following me. Haven't you done enough?!"

"Molly, I'm sorry."

"Just go away!"

Molly's phone buzzed. She looked at it, frowned, and handed it to me, "It's for you."

On the screen was a text from MLE with a link. I punched the link. . . .

It was a video of me at the arcade. I looked like a dork. I looked like someone I would laugh at and then get other kids to laugh at. Just like *that* kid at *that* school. Just like . . .

"Please go," pleaded Molly.

I looked down. Phil was leading Memaw and

Mr. Dupree up the stairs. I looked up. Simone had reached the top and was putting on a zip-line harness.

I looked at the video again. Maybe Simone had a point. Maybe running away and pretending to be from France was the answer. Maybe there *aren't* worse things than exposing your principal's Deathicorn chest tattoo . . . or hanging from a hippo head in your underwear above your entire class.

Maybe by the time I repeat seventh grade, everyone will have forgotten. Maybe.

But probably not.

I handed Molly back her phone and started down the stairs.

"Thin . . . air . . . hard . . . to breathe . . . Next . . . time . . . bring . . . oxygen."

"Karl?" I said.

I looked down. Karl was wheezing, three flights below. What was he doing? He couldn't be up here.

"Karl? You're afraid—"

"Of . . . heights?" gasped Karl. "I . . . know. It's my . . . number one . . . fear. But when . . . I saw Molly . . . looked . . . hurt—"

"You ran."

"Yeah. Weird."

Karl looked down, shuddered, and quickly looked back up. "Is she okay?"

I shook my head. "She found out Simone is *that* kid from *that* school."

"Simone was chased by scorpions in her boxer-briefs?"

"No. Simone was the principal's-sleeve-on-fire-Deathicorn-tattoo one."

"So the scorpions are fine?"

"What? I don't . . . It doesn't matter!" I said as I started down the stairs again. "Simone's just going to run to some other school and pretend she's from Australia or Chile . . . or wherever."

"Did you know there's a turtle from Australia that can breathe through its butt?"

I stopped. "What?"

"You said Australia, and I thought of butt-breathing turtles."

"Who does that?"

I shook my head. "You're so strange."

"You think I'm strange?"

"I mean, you're Karl. That's who you are. Who else would you be?"

"Who else would I be? Sometimes I think about being an Olympic Twister champ, and once I thought I'd like to have fins, but that's all just pretend. In the real world, if I wasn't who I am, I wouldn't be in Safety Patrol with you and Molly."

Wait. Memaw was right!

I want to be taller. Molly wants to be shorter. Becky wants to be plainer. Simone wants to be less Internet-famous. We ALL just want to be normal.

Except for Karl.

We just want to blend in. But Karl's completely cool with sticking out.

Karl looked up at Molly. "I know something that'll cheer her up. I'll tell her my parakeet, Stanley, now poops every time you look at him. It's gross. But a really cool kind of gross."

Karl was right. If we don't stick out, how can we stick together?

"Nick! Karl! Stay right where you are," yelled Phil from below. "We're almost there."

I looked up. Simone was in her harness and about to step off the platform.

I turned to Karl. "I've got to go. Can you stay with Molly?"

"Sure. But where are you going?

I started up the stairs.

CHAPTER 31

By the time I got to the top of the pyramid, Simone was far ahead, flying down the zip line. To catch up I was going to have to fly faster. But how? I looked around for something, anything, that would make me zip faster.

Then (after praying there weren't any more cell phone cameras pointed my way) I looked down the stairs.

Phil, Memaw, and Mr. Dupree had reached Karl and Molly. Phil looked up and spotted me. "STOP!" he yelled.

Too late. I'd already stepped off the platform and into thin air. That's when I screamed. Not out of fear. Out of pain. The harness punched me *WAY* below the belt.

After I'd readjusted the harness, I looked ahead. Simone was still a ways away, but I was closing in FAST.

I was closing in TOO fast. At the rate I was going, we were going to collide at the base of Crocodile Falls.

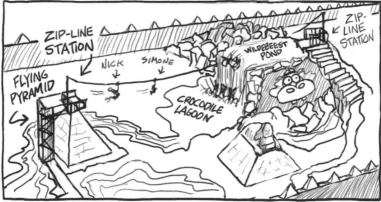

"Simone! Watch out!" I screamed.

Simone looked back. Her eyes popped. "What?! You?! STOP!" she yelled.

But I couldn't stop.

I looked ahead toward the falls just as the fake wildebeest was about to tumble over to the waiting fake crocodiles below.

If we didn't do something, Simone and I were going to collide, fall, and get fake—eaten alive!!

Simone scrambled to get out of her harness. "Jump!" she screamed.

I started throwing off the extra helmets and tearing at the harnesses until I heard a . . .

I yanked the last strap and . . .

I got snagged by Simone's harness! I tugged and pulled, but it was no use. I was stuck.

Simone looked up at me as she and the lagoon slid past. "NORMAL IS OVERRATED!" I yelled.

She shook her head and mouthed, *What*?

The roar of Crocodile Falls drowned her out. I looked down to see the fake crocodiles tearing into the fake wildebeest, and I knew it was all over.

Simone was gone. And I was going to repeat seventh grade. I stopped struggling and accepted my fate.

Of course, I probably should've checked with fate first. . . .

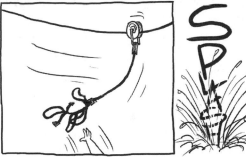

Somehow the harness released me. When I surfaced, I knew something was wrong.

I turned and saw I was headed straight for . . .

I'm *not* a bad kid! What did fate have against me?

MICHAEL FRY

spent middle school as a geeky, nerdy Chess Club member who played the French horn—and loved every minute of it (well, most minutes).

His school days behind him, Mike is the author of the Odd Squad series and the co-creator and writer of several comic strips, including *Over the Hedge*, which is featured in newspapers nationwide and was adapted into the hit animated movie of the same name. In addition to working as a cartoonist, Mike was a cofounder of RingTales, a company that animates print comics for all digital media, and is an active blogger, tweeter, and public speaker, as well as the proud father of two adult daughters.

Originally from Minneapolis, Mike currently lives with his wife in Austin, Texas, where he is hard at work on the next Odd Squad adventure.

Visit him online at www.oddsquadbooks.com.

ACKNOWLEDGMENTS

Writing this second book in the Odd Squad series was fun but scary. The first book, *Bully Bait*, was so well received that I fretted over whether I could do it again. To the extent I've succeeded, I'd like to thank my editor, Lisa Yoskowitz, for patiently and expertly guiding me to completion. It's a long road to publication, and it helps to have someone say over and over again, "You're almost done!" Except, when Lisa says it, it's more like "You'realmostdone!"

I'd also like to thank my agent, Dan Lazar. Dan is that calm voice on the other end of the line describing in vivid detail exactly what will happen should I step off the ledge I have repeatedly found myself on. He may have missed his calling as a hostage negotiator.

There are many, many friends who contributed to the book. Too many to mention (you're all mentioned in the first book; don't be greedy). Except for Kevin. Kevin's contribution was cut. So not mentioning him would be petty. Not that I'm above being petty, but it really means a lot to him. Probably too much, but let's not get into that here.

My wife and daughters were as supportive as ever. Which is to say, I'm still married, and the girls are still speaking to me.

Finally, a special thanks to our dog, Jack. During our launch party he was sequestered in my studio above the garage. He so wanted to join the celebration that he leapt out an open window resulting in a broken leg (and a serious hit to our bank account).

Here's to Jack—my biggest fan.

KAREN CUSHMAN was born in Chicago and moved to California with her family when she was ten. She now lives on Vashon Island, west of Seattle, with her husband, Philip.

Ms. Cushman is the author of the Newbery Medal book *The Midwife's Apprentice*, the Newbery Honor book *Catherine, Called Birdy*, and *Matilda Bone*, all set in medieval England. Francine Green is the third Cushman protagonist whose story is set in the USA, joining Rodzina ("prickly but endearing" —*School Library Journal*, starred; "a delightful, thoroughly Polish heroine"—*The New York Times* Book Review) and Lucy Whipple ("an irresistible teenager"—*Kirkus Reviews*, pointer).

I swam as hard as I could, but the current was too strong. I grasped for anything: a branch, a rock, a horn.

A horn?

Miraculously, I'd gotten hold of the wildebeest at the top of the falls. I was saved!

So, technically, I was still saved. For three minutes!

I looked left and right. I couldn't swim to either shore without going over the falls first.

I looked up. The zip line was about six feet above me.

If I could stand up, I could grab the zip line and go hand over hand until I was clear of the pond.

It was a perfect plan, except for three things.

It looked hopeless, but I had to try.

I crouched in position, rising and falling in the current a foot each way. By timing the rise, I could just reach the zip cord. I started to count. One . . . two . . .

"What?! You?!" I cried.

"This doesn't mean I don't still sort of hate you," said Molly.

"Then why . . . ?"

"Karl filled me in. Nobody's been willing to repeat seventh grade for me before."

"Nick! Just hang on a little longer!"

I turned around. It was Memaw. She was with Mr. Dupree, Phil, and the field-trip kids at the zip-line station, waiting for us.

"You'll be safe soon!" yelled Memaw.

"Is Simone gone forever?" asked Karl.

I turned back around. "She's probably going to leave for another school now that her secret's out," I said.

Molly had that look on her face like when NanoNerd lost his NanoCat in the Spleen Swamps of Smot. Kinda sad, yet brave.

I said, "There'll be other . . . friends that . . . I mean . . . are not . . . you know. . . just us."

Molly nodded. "I know." Then she took a deep breath and smiled. "In the meantime, I guess I can still be friends with you two."

"Great!" I said.

"Huzzah!" yelled Karl.

"There's just one condition."

"Name it," I said.

NO MORE HUGGING!

CHAPTER 32

An hour later, I stared at Perfect Phil, sitting across from me. Dr. Daniels stood behind him. She looked like she wanted to be somewhere else. I knew exactly how she felt.

Phil opened a thick binder and started reading. "Bullying, video and audio recording a student without permission, making false accusations, failure to honor a suspension, attending a restricted school event, failure to heed a faculty

member's orders . . . impersonating a costumed character . . ."

"Seriously?" I said.

"Seriously. But the only one that matters is bullying. This is your second incident, Nick. You know what comes next."

Mom leaned forward. "Nick was just trying to do the right thing." She turned to me and glared. "In as stupid and dangerous a way as possible!"

Phil shook his head. "I'm sorry. I really am."

"That Simone girl set Nick up," said Memaw. "She was *trying* to get him expelled, because she didn't want anyone to know she sets principals on fire."

I turned around. Simone was standing at the door with her dad.

"And I'm not from France." She looked at me.

"I didn't mean to hurt you. It's just that after everything that happened I—"

"Just wanted to be normal?" I said.

Simone nodded.

Memaw said, "How does pretending to be French or getting Nick suspended have anything to do with being normal? It doesn't make any sense!"

"It makes sense to me," I said.

I looked at Simone. "Now that everyone knows what happened, I figured you'd take off for another school. Why'd you come back?"

"I thought about what you said."

"Normal is overrated?"

"No. What you said in that basement Safety Patrol meeting a couple weeks ago."

I shook my head.

"You said, 'She hasn't been trained. She hasn't been bullied. She's not . . .'" Simone whispered, "'. . . one of us.'"

"Oh. Right," I said.

"But when I saw that you couldn't tell Molly the truth about me and how Karl put his fear aside to be with a friend and how both Molly and Karl rescued you and how YOU . . ."

She handed me her phone. It was another video from MLE.

I looked up. "How . . . ?"

Karl nodded. "Emily is *everywhere*."

Simone continued, "You risked years of online video torture to try to invite me to the party."

"The party?" I said. "How did you know about—?"

"A one-headed chicken is normal," said Molly.

"But a two-headed chicken is a lot more fun at parties," added Karl.

I turned to Memaw. She shrugged. "We text."

"You were right," said Simone. "I'm not like all of you. I'm *way* too normal."

BUT I CAN CHANGE.

"I don't know who this Emily is or what two-headed chickens have to do with anything," said Phil. "The fact remains that Nick bullied Simone twice, and Zero Tolerance dictates—"

Mom interrupted, "But Simone just admitted to—"

"Zero Tolerance is the law of the school," continued Phil. "And because it's the law—"

"Wait. That's it!" I said. "What if ZT isn't the law?!"

"But it is," said Phil. "It became the law because *you* were bullied."

"But what if I wasn't bullied?" I said.

"Nick, you were wrapped in TP and stuffed in a trash can," said Dr. Daniels.

I looked down. "I . . . um . . . bullied myself," I whispered.

"What?!" cried Mom and Memaw.

Time to come clean.

Phil shook his head. "I still don't see why any of this new information matters. What matters is—"

"No one was bullied!" I interrupted. "ZT didn't need to be the law. So anything that happened after that can't be under ZT!"

Phil smiled. "Nice try, Nick, but—"

"Fruit of the poisonous tree!" cried Memaw. "Like on that show *Justice and Peace*. That squirrelly defense lawyer is always screaming, 'Fruit of the poisonous tree!'"

"What?" said Phil.

"Oh, you don't want to eat those," said Karl. "I know. My mom had to buy me all new underwear."

"No," said Dr. Daniels. "It means any bullying that happens under a false application of Zero Tolerance is not under Zero Tolerance."

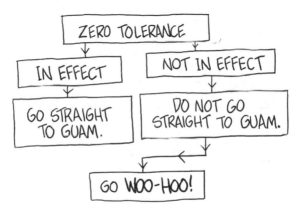

"Woo-hoo!" I cheered.

"That's *not* what it means!" said Phil.

"Are you sure?" said Dr. Daniels.

Memaw took out her phone.

WHAT'S THE NAME OF THAT LAWYER? THE ONE WITH NO UPPER LIP.

Dr. Daniels said, "I think the best course of action is to put the Zero Tolerance program on hold pending a review by the school board."

"Excellent idea," said Memaw as she put away her phone.

Phil looked stunned. "But . . ."

Molly, Karl, Simone, and I cheered.

It was awesome. Everybody got what they wanted. Well, everybody except Phil.

As everyone started to leave the office, Perfect Phil flashed his perfect smile and approached my mom.

"We're still good, right?" he asked.

"Phil, I don't think we should see each other anymore."

CHAPTER 33

J ust because Simone didn't have to move again and I didn't have to repeat seventh grade didn't mean we didn't get punished. After all, Simone did try to get me expelled and I did fake-bully myself.

At first I thought Dr. Daniels was going to sentence us to bossy-girl prison with six weeks of Peer Mediation. But Mr. Dupree suggested a different idea.

223

Meanwhile, Becky gave up gum. She sort of had to.

Simone returned Karl's beret and also suggested he wear a scarf. She thought it would make him look *très chic*! Everyone teases him. But Karl's got a thick skin that repels all insults.

It's sort of like a superpower, only more useful.

My mom's taking a break from dating. Which

is fine by me. It gives me a chance to recover from all the fake smiling and pretend niceness.

Then there's Molly. She'd saved my life twice in three weeks, and I owed her a lot. But how could I repay her? I couldn't help her with school, since she's way smarter than me. I could be nicer to her, but that would get weird really fast.

I didn't know what to do, so I asked Memaw.

She said, "Write her a thank-you note like the ones you never write me."

I thought, What if I *draw* her a thank-you note?

So I did. I drew her a NanoNerd thank-you note:

She loved it. I could tell, because she was speechless.

Afterward, we stood around for what seemed like forever and tried not to say anything that would cause either of us to barf.

Finally, after enough time had passed (six seconds), I said, "Where's Karl?"

Molly shrugged. "It's not my day to watch him."

"Wait," I said as I pulled out my phone. "I know how to find him. Karl's Beret-Cam still works. I had the feed forwarded to my phone."

"You spy on him?"

"It was his idea. In case he's attacked by plastic bags or mummies or costumed characters or—"

"Antique furniture."

"Right. I never look at it. It's mostly just video of the boys' bathroom and sea monkeys."

I brought up the feed on my phone. "Wait. What?"

"What is it?"

227

"Karl's holding some sort of invitation. And it's from MLEZ!"

"MLEZ? Like there's more than one?"

"Emily is a WE!" I cried.

"Who are *they*?!"

I looked at Molly. "And what do they want with Karl?"

I could tell Molly and I were thinking the same thing.

MLEZ + = A SUPER SECRET FREAK FORCE THAT CAN CONTROL THE SCHOOL!

That's when Molly and I both realized that for every no-hugging rule, there was one exception:

KARL COULD CONTROL THE SCHOOL!!

AHHHHHHH